The Travelers Detective Club

PARIS

SUSSI VOAK

ISBN -13 978-1-7340093-2-3

Cover illustration by Dede Nugraha

Chapter heading design by S. M. Savoy

DEDICATION

To Laura F and Laura P for helping me uncover my inner writer and for your unwavering support and encouragement.

Table of Contents

1. Getting Ready

Ever wake up to a live magical creature jumping up and down on your face? It was not the first time for Jeremy Johnson, and he wasn't amused.

"Get …" boing, "up …" boing, "sleepy …" boing, "head." Boing. Jeremy's arm flailed through the air, trying to grab Thing, but this was difficult to do with his eyes closed. He opened his eyes and realized Thing punctuated each word with a midair somersault. With his last bounce, Thing landed on the bed.

Thing was a pint-sized orange ball of fur, just smaller than a grapefruit. He had big beady eyes but no mouth, short arms with large hands, feet but no legs, and a tail. Orange strands of hair stuck straight up, mohawk like, on the top of his head.

"Jeremy!" his mom called from outside his door. "Time to get up."

"Told … you." Thing emphasized each word by bouncing on Jeremy's face before performing a midair jumping jack.

"Alright, alright. But I'm going to get you back for that." Jeremy yanked the covers off and sat at the edge of the bed. He stared at the clothes piled on his floor, grabbed a stray sock at his feet and hurled it at Thing, who was resting on a shelf above his bed, where he'd landed after his last aerial maneuver.

The sock, though headed straight for Thing, stopped in midair and dropped back to the bed. "Good thing you don't play baseball," Thing said. "And please, wash your feet will ya."

Thing was a magic buddy, sent to Jeremy in a box with a note inducting him into the Travelers Detective Club. A magic buddy's main responsibility was to help find clues, which Thing did on their trip to Portugal the previous summer. Thing could change color: red when another detective was nearby, yellow if Jeremy was moving away from a clue, blue when near a clue, and purple if there was danger. In Portugal, Thing also provided comic relief, pretending to swim when tethered to the side of Jeremy's leg and teasing Jeremy whenever possible. Thing loved to make comments about Jeremy's ability, or lack thereof, to solve the mystery they were assigned.

Jeremy chuckled, stood up and scanned his room, taking in the general disorderliness. He realized he probably should have done more the previous night to get ready. His mind wandered to the email he'd received just last week, and smiled.

Dear Jeremy,

I'm so excited that we get to hang out again this summer, even

if just for a few days. I've always wanted to go to Paris and stand under the Eiffel Tower. And I can't wait to go to the Louvre. I've heard you could spend weeks there and never see it all.

Birdbrain is still incorrigible. I'm not sure what to do though I guess I can't really do anything, can I? I've had to stop taking her out, cause she almost gets caught–flapping her wings and making noises–people are always looking at me funny. It's embarrassing. Anyway, perhaps we'll get to go on an adventure when we're in France, and she can put her energy into something useful.

See you in a few days,

Devon

P.S. Is it a coincidence that Tech is sending both our parents to Paris?

Birdbrain was Devon's magic buddy, a small, bird-like stuffed animal with an oversized beak and feathers that stuck out at odd angles. She had been afraid of heights and ashamed of it, causing her to be very subdued the previous summer. After getting over her fear at the end of the trip, Birdbrain had hardly been able to contain herself, flapping her wings and yelling "whee" loud enough that people took notice.

Magic buddies were expected to be quiet and inconspicuous. The general public wasn't supposed to know they were magical. Jeremy had known Devon would have her hands full, and it served her right. She'd snickered and chuckled at the antics of Thing, even suggesting he and Thing deserved each other.

Thing was a bundle of energy, sarcasm, and wit. He seemed to like nothing more than to drive Jeremy crazy, which he'd done often over the course of the school year. He liked to hide things from Jeremy, even rearrange his entire room, when stuck inside.

"I can't take you to school," Jeremy told Thing a million times. "Kids will make fun of me. I know you're cool and awesome and magical, but they can't know that. They'll just think I'm carrying around a little kids' toy. I'd get laughed right off the schoolyard."

For all the times Jeremy reminded Thing why he had to stay home, Thing expressed his displeasure by messing up Jeremy's room. This included hanging Jeremy's underwear on the corners of posters and hiding all of his pencils and pens, making it difficult for Jeremy to do his homework. The worst was when he emptied a box of Cheerios under the sheets in Jeremy's bed.

Jeremy got up and found his favorite pair of jeans on the floor. He started tossing clothes from his drawers into his half-packed suitcase, pausing to put on his new navy blue t-shirt. "DON'T TOUCH MY HAIR" was on the front and "JUST DON'T" on the back. When he and his mom traveled, strangers would reach out and touch his tight black curls; he tried to duck but couldn't always avoid them.

It was annoying enough that people stared at him and his mom. Jeremy, who was black, was adopted, and his mom was white. She adopted him on her own, so it was just the two of them. One day, after he had endured ten different attempts to touch his head, his mom searched online until she found this shirt. He wondered if it would help.

"Jeremy. Breakfast."

"Okay," he shouted back.

The smell of eggs and bacon drifted into his room. "Come on, Thing. Time to go."

"You know, you could just shave your head."

"I could just shave you."

"Good point. As I was saying, nice shirt." Thing allowed Jeremy to clip him to a carabiner on his backpack, and Jeremy traipsed downstairs.

His mom's cell phone rang as he hit the bottom step. An urgency in her voice made Jeremy pause on his way to the kitchen. Standing just outside of view, he strained to hear her almost whispered words.

"... stolen? I thought that was impossible. So it's started.... Yeah, good thing we're there later today. Do I need to cancel my day tomorrow? ... No? ... You sure? Okay."

Jeremy stepped into the kitchen.

"Jeremy, I need you to hurry up. We're going to be late."
His mom placed a plate of eggs, bacon and toast on the
counter.

"What was stolen?"

He had clearly caught his mom off guard. "Nothing," she
said, turning her back. "Just something from work."

Jeremy sat down at the counter and slid his fried eggs and
bacon onto a piece of toast. "You're always getting us places
early."

"We're meeting Cheryl and Sam at the airport, and I don't
want to be late."

Jeremy rolled his eyes.

"And don't roll your eyes like that." Jeremy hadn't realized
she'd turned back around.

Jeremy slapped a second piece of toast over his eggs,
causing his plate to tip and slam onto the counter. He took a
large bite of his sandwich.

His mom wiped down the kitchen counters. "I know this is
hard for you, but Cheryl is very important to me and—"

"What about me?" Jeremy grumbled to himself. His words
were incoherent, because his mouth was full.

"What?" His mom narrowed her eyes, and he recognized that she was both questioning him and calling him out for talking with his mouth full.

Jeremy swallowed. He hated feeling left out, like he wasn't always number one, and that was Cheryl's fault. But he didn't want to hurt his mom's feelings.

"Jeremy?"

"Why couldn't Sam just stay with his other mom?"

Jeremy's mom rinsed the rag she used to wipe the counters. "We've been over this Jeremy. Both Cheryl and I thought it would be good for you boys to get to know each other better. Plus, it's Paris, and you both want to go."

When Jeremy didn't acknowledge her, but stared at his plate, she continued. "Come on. It's Paris."

Jeremy sighed, eyeing his mom. "Okay," he said halfheartedly.

His mom's phone buzzed. "Our ride is here."

Jeremy grabbed his bags and followed his mom outside. He slammed the door on the way out.

2. The Airport

Jeremy positioned his backpack in the car so Thing could have a view out the window. He knew Thing would complain if he didn't.

If Jeremy was honest with his mom, he'd admit to being scared about going to Paris with Cheryl and Sam. This trip meant that their relationship was getting serious. It had always been just Jeremy and his mom, and he wasn't sure he was ready for it to be different. Sam was actually kind of fun to hang out with, Jeremy grudgingly admitted to himself. He sighed.

"What?" Thing whispered.

Jeremy ignored him.

"Grouch," Thing muttered.

Jeremy pulled out his headphones. He'd downloaded some new music for the trip the night before: a new hip hop album and an up and coming pop artist, his eclectic taste in music reflecting the diversity of his life.

Thirty minutes later, they were standing curbside at the airport. Once inside, Jeremy and his mom got in line to check their bags. Ten minutes later, Sam and his mom joined them.

Sam had a new crew cut and clearly cared about color coordinating his wardrobe; his backpack, shoes, and shirt were all red and black. Jeremy's mom gave Cheryl a kiss. Trying to ignore his insides, Jeremy turned up the music on his MP3. Moments later his mom tapped his arm. He peeled his Beats off, his music still audible.

"Turn that down, Jeremy. You'll ruin your ears. And can you please say hi?" His mom's face said both please and you darn well better at the same time. How did she do that?

"Hi," Jeremy said, barely looking at Cheryl.

"Hi, Jeremy," Cheryl said.

Jeremy started to put his headphones back on.

"Turn it down, Jeremy," his mom repeated. "And did you say hi to Sam?"

Jeremy glanced at Sam. "Hey."

"Hi," Sam replied.

After a look from his mom, Jeremy turned his music off but kept to himself. Once their bags were checked, they trudged down to security. When it was their turn, a TSA agent told Jeremy to take off his shoes.

"He's twelve," his mom intervened. "He doesn't have to take off his shoes."

"Take off your shoes," the woman repeated to Jeremy, ignoring his mom.

Jeremy looked at his mom.

She nodded. "Go ahead."

While Jeremy removed his shoes, his mom confronted the woman. She pointed to Sam. "You didn't ask him to take his shoes off. They're the same age."

The woman ignored her and proceeded to give general reminders out loud to the crowd.

The airport was packed, and Jeremy began to feel self-conscious; the man next to them froze in the middle of taking off his belt. Others stood watching, shoes in hands, jackets half off.

"Forget it, Mom."

Sam went through the old style x-ray detector followed by Cheryl. Jeremy stepped up next, but a different TSA agent directed him toward the full body scanner.

Jeremy's mom stepped forward. "Excuse me. He's with me, and he's only twelve."

Jeremy squirmed. He really didn't want to be the center of attention.

"We always go through this one." His mom pointed to the x-ray machine.

"Oh, he's with you?" the man said. "Okay." And he motioned Jeremy through after Sam.

"What's going on, Jess?" Cheryl asked.

"They're giving Jeremy a hard time." Her eyes were glistening.

"It's okay, Mom," Jeremy said half-heartedly. He was starting to feel not only annoyance, but shame.

"No, Jeremy, it's not."

"What's going on?" Sam asked.

"Can we just get out of here and go to the gate?" Jeremy wanted to put as much distance between himself and this scene, these people, as possible.

Once at the gate, they found seats and settled in. Jeremy had his headphones back on and his eyes closed, though the conversation next to him was still audible.

"I'm sorry, Jess," Cheryl said.

"What's the big deal?" Sam asked. "So he had to take off his shoes."

"Sam," Jeremy's mom said, "Jeremy was asked to take his shoes off and go through the scanner because he's black. Twelve-year-olds don't have to remove their shoes. But white people often think black kids are older than they are and dangerous for no reason."

"Oh," Sam said.

"Cheryl, you did remind him how his behavior could get Jeremy in trouble, right?"

"Yeah, she did," Sam said. "But I don't really get it."

Jeremy opened his eyes.

"I'm not sure how it will be in Paris," Jeremy's mom began. "Your mom reminded you that in the states, black people are treated with suspicion, right?"

Sam nodded.

"That's why we don't have Nerf guns at our house. Someone might call the cops saying that Jeremy has a gun, when they would never do that to you. So in Paris, if you and Jeremy are horsing around and being too loud, someone might reprimand Jeremy but not you. "

"So we need you to be mindful of how your actions might impact Jeremy," Cheryl finished.

Jeremy turned his music up.

3. Welcome to Paris

Jeremy walked back to his seat on the plane, head down, music blaring. He stuffed his backpack underneath the seat in front of him and looked out the window. Sam sat down next to him. Jeremy didn't feel like interacting. He hated being treated differently. And why were they talking about it now? Shouldn't Sam know all this? He sensed his mom's gaze on him from her seat across the aisle but ignored her. She should know he didn't want to be the center of attention.

Once the plane took off, and the sky wasn't enough of a distraction, Jeremy grabbed an inflight magazine from the pocket in front of him. Something fell out onto the floor. He reached down and grabbed the metal, irregularly shaped object. It was a miniature golden Eiffel Tower on a keychain.

"What's that?" Sam asked.

Jeremy took off his headphones. "Don't know. Something I found on the floor. Just a keychain is all."

"Oh." Sam pulled a Nintendo Switch from his bag.

Darn, he has a Switch? Jeremy rubbed his head and sighed.

Sam must have noticed because he said, "Wanna play?"

Jeremy was bent over, attempting to put the trinket away in his backpack. His determination to take his anger out on Sam conflicted with his desire to play video games. While he paused, something jabbed his foot. He glanced down, receiving a glare from Thing, whom Jeremy, in his grumpiness, forgot about when tucking his backpack under the seat. Thing was blue. A clue must be nearby.

"Um, yeah." Jeremy sat up. "Just give me a minute."

"Okay." Sam started playing on his own.

Jeremy bent back down, unclipped Thing, mouthed, "Sorry," and placed him on the seat next to him. Jeremy examined the miniature Eiffel Tower. A piece of paper tucked into its base caught his eye.

Sam seemed engrossed in his game, so Jeremy pulled out the note, unfolded it, and noticed the TDC emblem emblazoned at the top. The message below was short: *7:30 pm tomorrow, 59th floor, Tour Montparnasse.* Jeremy's heart pounded in his chest. Who was meeting him? Not just him. Devon would be there too. Did Travis send this note? Would they get to wander around Paris, solving another mystery like they did in Portugal? Jeremy tucked the note and trinket in his backpack.

How could he have forgotten about the Travelers Detective Club? He'd been preoccupied, that's how. Mom dating … oh, Sam. What about him? He's not in the club. Jeremy glanced over at him, absorbed in his game. Who cares. He and Devon would figure it out. And the stupid agents at the airport … Jeremy closed his eyes and took a deep breath. They didn't deserve his energy.

Jeremy joined Sam on his Switch and they alternated between games and movies playing on their individual TV screens. Jeremy's mood lightened more, and he forgot to take his anger out on Sam.

After landing and going through customs in the Paris airport, they headed to baggage claim. Jeremy glimpsed a man over six feet tall, his shaved head and mocha colored skin standing out against the sea of mostly white tourists. What was Travis doing here? And thank goodness there was another black person. Jeremy never mentioned it out loud, but being the only black person in a room made him feel out of place.

Jeremy met Travis in Portugal during his first adventure with the Travelers Detective Club. Jeremy wished his initial encounter with Travis had been different. He'd assumed Travis was a threat when he caught sight of him at Saint George's Castle. But Travis had sent him his magic buddy as one of the few adults in charge of the TDC.

Before Jeremy could say anything, Travis spoke to his mom. "Ms. Johnson. Welcome to Paris. How was your flight?"

"Hi, Mr. Davis," she said, shaking his hand. "It was good, thanks. It's so nice of you to meet us here."

During this exchange, Jeremy gazed back and forth between his mom and Travis. He caught Travis's eye for a moment. Travis shook his head ever so slightly.

"This is my son, Jeremy," his mom said.

"Nice to meet you." Travis reached out his hand, and Jeremy took it, his mind whirling. "I am the head of human resources for Tech," Travis said.

"Oh, okay," Jeremy stammered. "Well, thanks for meeting us."

His mom introduced Cheryl and Sam.

"I'll apologize ahead of time for all the meetings that will keep Jess busy," Travis said. "But we'll try and give her some time off."

"So, are you our welcoming committee?" Jeremy's mom smiled.

"Sure, if you'd like to call me that. Though more importantly, I'm your ride to the hotel."

Twenty minutes later Cheryl and Sam had their bags. Jeremy's mom and Travis were in the airline's lost and found office to inquire about Jeremy's and her bags. In the glass-walled office, his mom opened her backpack before turning away. Jeremy could have sworn she handed something to Travis, though she seemed intent on hiding that fact.

"Everything okay, Mom?" he asked as she walked back to him.

Her eyes darted to Travis before she spoke. "They seem to have lost our luggage. Sent it somewhere else. They're hoping to deliver it to us tomorrow."

Jeremy walked behind his mom and Travis on their way to the car. Both of them were looking around a lot. His mom was acting strangely, but Jeremy stayed quiet. Once in the car, Jeremy gazed out the window, lost in thought and not taking in any scenery. Thing kicked Jeremy to remind him he wanted to stare out the window.

"What's that?" Sam asked, pointing at Thing.

"Oh, it's nothing," Jeremy replied, ensuring he blocked Sam's view of Thing.

Thing widened his eyes at Jeremy.

"Sorry," Jeremy mouthed at Thing, but Thing ignored him and gazed out the window.

They arrived at their hotel and went up to the fifth floor. "Tech has rented several hotel rooms and suites in this building," Travis explained. "You're staying here." They were outside room 505. "And Bob and his family will be next door."

"Bob?" Jeremy asked.

"Devon's dad," his mom reminded him.

"Oh, right. Cool. When do they get here?"

"Tomorrow," Travis replied. He handed Jess and Cheryl each a key card. "I'll leave you here so you can get settled in. Tomorrow night at six o'clock there's a dinner for everyone at Le Ciel de Paris in the Tour Montparnasse. If you need anything, don't hesitate to track me down then."

Once inside the hotel suite, Jeremy's mom pointed to the room with two twin beds. "Okay, you two. Go check out your room. Unpack, use the bathroom, whatever, because we're heading out in ten minutes."

"Where are we going?" Sam asked.

"Out," his mom replied. "The best way to get through jet lag is to try and stay up, so we're going to go check out the neighborhood. There's only one rule." She smiled at Jess.

"What?" Jeremy and Sam asked at the same time.

"You guys are in charge of where we go. And you have to decide together."

Jeremy and Sam looked at each other. Jeremy shrugged and Sam smiled.

"Okay," said Jeremy.

"Sure," said Sam.

It was quiet in the room as the boys each threw their bags on a bed. Jeremy went into the bathroom. When he came out, he overheard Cheryl asking his mom if everything was alright. His mom started to say something, but when Jeremy and Sam came out of the bedroom, she stopped.

"Ready?" his mom said.

Once outside, Cheryl asked, "Which way?"

"Left," said Jeremy.

"Right," Sam said at the same time. They eyed each other for a moment before Sam said, "Let's roshambo for it."

"What?" Jeremy asked.

"Rock-paper-scissors."

"Oh, right."

They counted to three, and Sam's paper smothered Jeremy's rock, so they turned right. They took their time walking down the sun-drenched streets, wandering down narrow lanes paved in stones and lined with off-white stone buildings, four and five stories tall. They passed storefronts with colorful green and red awnings, cafes with people sitting at outdoor tables sipping coffee from miniature cups, flower shops with buckets of roses, tulips, and other flowers Jeremy didn't recognize. Ten minutes or so of exploring brought them to an entrance to the Jardin du Luxembourg. Strolling down tree-lined paths made of crushed stone, they passed multiple life-size statues and beds of flowers surrounding plots of grass. They stopped to watch children sail tiny boats on a miniature lake that lay in front of Luxembourg Palace. Eventually they ended up near an enclosed playground the size of a football field. On the edge, kids of different ages swung around on a circular zipline. Sam and Jeremy eyed each other.

Jeremy tilted his head toward the park. "You game?"

"Sure," Sam said.

"Hey, Mom," they both called out at the same time.

Jeremy continued, "It's my turn, and I say that we go in there."

"Really?" his mom said. "Aren't you a bit—"

Jeremy pointed to a sign at the entrance. "Up to age sixteen, Mom. No, I'm not too old."

"Okay, okay," his mom laughed.

The boys raced to the zipline, Sam just beating Jeremy. While they waited in line, Jeremy's mom and Cheryl strolled close together to a nearby bench.

"Still not used to it, huh?" Sam remarked.

"What?"

"Our moms, together." Sam stepped up to the zipline seat. "You're still not used to it." Sam pushed off from the platform.

Jeremy went next, swinging around in a wide arc. He jumped off and caught up with Sam. "No, actually I'm not. What about you?"

"Well, yeah, I guess." Sam wandered toward a giant tree fort. "I mean, my Mama Diane has had a girlfriend for about a year, and I just figured Mom would eventually find someone."

"When did your parents separate?" Jeremy climbed a ladder up into the fort.

"When I was eight. It was awful, and I was so mad. I still get mad sometimes, but what can I do?"

"It's always just been Mom and me." Jeremy stopped at the top of the ladder and stared off into the distance.

From the fort, he could look down on the surrounding area. Someone approached their moms from behind. The hairs on the back of Jeremy's neck tingled. Whomever it was appeared to be trying to sneak up on them. "Mom, watch out!"

"What, Jeremy?"

While her attention was on Jeremy, the person reached down and grabbed her backpack resting on the bench between her and Cheryl. His mom reached to grab it but was too late. While she stood up and started running after the thief, Jeremy jumped off the fort and ran through the entrance to the park. He caught up to his mom who had abandoned her chase. "He was too fast," she said.

Walking back to their hotel, Jeremy's mom seemed rattled. She hardly said anything, which was the case when she was overly stressed and had a lot on her mind.

"Was there anything important in your backpack?" Cheryl asked. They passed the miniature lake with its multitude of sailboats.

"No, thank goodness. I thought I was being careful but apparently not enough."

First their luggage went missing and then he saw his mom give Travis something at the airport. Was it just a coincidence that his mom's backpack had been stolen?

4. The Eiffel Tower

Back at their hotel, Sam was the first one out of the elevator. "Mom, did you forget to close the door?"

"What?"

Jeremy stepped past Sam. Sure enough, the door was ajar. That's weird. He started to walk into the room when his mom grabbed his arm. "Don't go in. I'm sure I closed the door. Someone could be in there. We need to go down to security."

After hotel security ensured it was empty, Jeremy followed his mom and Cheryl into the suite. Cheryl's and Sam's suitcases had been rifled through, their clothes thrown about the two rooms. Jeremy's backpack had also been torn apart.

"How did they get in?" Cheryl asked.

Jeremy walked into their room. His mom was searching her pockets. "My key card was in my backpack."

"But how did they know this was our hotel room?" Cheryl pulled out the new key card she'd been issued by security. "The cards are blank."

Jeremy's mom shook her head. "I don't know, Cheryl."

Cheryl gasped. "Our passports." She opened her suitcase and checked an inside pocket. "Jess, they took our passports." Cheryl's voice cracked. "Something's weird here. I feel like we're being targeted. But why?"

"I don't know." Jeremy's mom spoke quietly, and her face was expressionless, but her hands were shaking.

Jeremy's mom was acting like she wasn't bothered but he'd never seen her hands tremble. Was she hiding something?

"Mom, what's going on?"

"I have no idea, Jeremy."

Jeremy didn't believe his mom for a minute but didn't press her. He bent down and picked up the miniature Eiffel Tower that someone pulled out of his backpack and dropped on the floor. He turned it over. The note in its base was missing.

In the morning, Jeremy woke up to voices from the next room. Sam was awake, and he put his index finger to his lips.

"Jess, the key cards don't have the room number on them, much less the name of the hotel. How could someone have known which room was ours? And why is someone so intent on searching our stuff?"

Silence.

"What aren't you telling me?" Cheryl said.

Jeremy and Sam heard footsteps approaching and immediately pretended to be asleep. The door to their room closed. The boys quietly got out of bed and put their ears to the door.

"My company monitors far-right extremist hate groups, one of which is active in Paris. It's possible they are shadowing us in turn."

"But they're more than following you," Cheryl said. "They're going through our stuff, looking for something…. Why didn't you think to tell me?"

Jeremy heard nothing for several moments. A ringing cut the silence. Cheryl answered the phone. A moment later she hung up. "They're delivering your luggage to the hotel by two o'clock." There was an iciness to her voice.

Jeremy's mom said, "Let's wake up the boys," prompting both of them to dive back into their beds.

An hour later they left for the metro station that would take them to the Eiffel Tower. Their moms hadn't talked much and the boys took their cues from them and kept quiet through breakfast. They walked in silence, Jeremy sensing a frostiness between Cheryl and his mom. They dodged Parisians hustling to work and other tourists strolling leisurely who were unknowingly blocking the path of those with somewhere to go. Up ahead, mouthwatering smells eased out of a bakery when the door opened and then swung shut.

"I think we could all use a treat," Jeremy's mom said.

"Sounds good to me." Jeremy opened the door and was hit with the smell of warm bread, chocolate and sugar. Loaves of bread lined up like books on a shelf. Decadent cakes covered in raspberries, strawberries and blueberries, miniature tarts glazed in sugar; chocolate, and jam-filled croissants, macaroons and many other unfamiliar pastries filled the displays. He had trouble making a decision but settled on a pain au chocolat and an éclair.

They ate their pastries while walking to the underground metro station. On the train, Jeremy realized the ridership was as diverse as that back home; he wasn't close to being the only person of color. He had been worried, at the airport, when most of the people picking up baggage were white.

At the third train stop, Bir-Hakem, they exited along with half of the train's passengers.

Strolling down the path on the side of the boulevard, Sam asked, "Are we close?"

"Look up." Jeremy pointed to the Eiffel Tower looming over them to their right.

"Oh," Sam said. "Dang, that's huge. How tall is it?"

"Nine hundred and eighty-four feet," Jeremy said. They weaved through groups of tourists gawking at the tower.

"That must have taken forever to build," Sam said.

"Not really. Two years, two months and five days is all."

"How do you know all that?"

"Looked it up the other day." Jeremy turned toward the base of the tower. The line to buy tickets for the elevator stretched around the corner, and they chose the stairs, since the wait was shorter.

As Jeremy climbed the steps, he paused occasionally to gaze at the city, creating space between him and the others.

"Not getting tired, are you?" Thing remarked. He hung from his carabiner clip attached to a loop on Jeremy's jeans.

"No. And you've been awfully quiet today."

"Did you just call me awful?" Thing asked.

"No, I didn't."

Thing pushed off Jeremy's leg. "Yes, you did."

"No, I did not. I mentioned that you had been quiet and used the word awfully as an adverb."

"What's an adverb?" Thing asked while doing a backflip.

"It's an ... oh never mind." Jeremy started up the stairs again.

"Well, serves you right. Having to walk up all these stairs instead of using the elevator ... calling me awful."

"Thing, I did not," Jeremy paused to catch his breath, "call ... you ... awful."

"Don't know why you're struggling. I'm not tired at all." Thing pretended to swim the backstroke.

Jeremy chuckled, feeling himself relax for the first time since he'd left home.

Once he arrived at the first level, Jeremy gazed to his left and then right, taking in the view of Paris below. A large, white, domed building rested on a hill in the distance. He edged up to his mom and pointed. "What's that?"

"That's the Sacré-Cœur. I'd like to go there while we're here."

"Cool…. Hey, is Cheryl still mad at you?"

His mom regarded him for a moment. "I'm not sure. We haven't had time to talk….You don't miss much do you?"

"Nope." He smiled before wandering to the other side of the platform.

"Look down," Thing said.

"What? Oh, wow." Jeremy's heart raced. He was standing on a glass floor. It was like standing on air. He continued to an opening in the crowd and peered over the edge. His gaze traveled to a clump of trees off to the side in an area devoid of tourists. Suddenly, one of them disappeared. "That's crazy," he mumbled.

"What's crazy?" Thing scrambled up as high as the carabineer allowed. "I mean, besides you." He jumped off Jeremy's leg.

Jeremy closed his eyes, took a deep breath and opened them again. Not being familiar with the view, he immediately doubted himself. He stared for a moment longer before rejoining his mom.

On their way back down from the second level, Thing baited Jeremy. "Can't you go any faster? Is there a reason you're so slow?"

"If you'd like, I can expedite your return to the ground by encouraging your free fall."

"You can expedite what? My free fall? Naw, I'm good."

"Thought so."

***

They stopped briefly at their apartment to change. Jeremy and his mom's luggage was delivered to the front desk while they were out. His mom must have found time to talk to Cheryl because the iciness between the two moms had disappeared. Taking the metro, they exited the Gare Montparnasse stop.

"That's impressive." Sam peered up at a skyscraper at least forty floors taller than the surrounding buildings.

"Tech has an office here and it's where I'll be for a good part of the week," Jeremy's mom said.

When they arrived at the restaurant on the fifty-sixth floor, a familiar voice called out from amongst a crowd of people. "Jeremy!"

Jeremy looked around and broke into a smile. "Devon!"

He walked to Devon and gave her a hug.

"We've only just got in," Devon said. "Our luggage was lost...." She inclined her head toward Sam who was now standing alone watching them. "Who's that?"

"Your luggage was lost?"

"Yeah, but it's no—"

"Our luggage was lost too," Jeremy said. "And get this ..." Jeremy proceeded to tell her about the day's happenings.

Sam wandered over as Jeremy finished his story.

Devon gave Sam a smile. "Hi, I'm Devon."

"Sam," he replied. "How do you know each other?"

"We met on a trip to Portugal," Devon replied. Her hazel eyes narrowed, surveying Jeremy. There were a dozen questions in her gaze.

"Sam and his mom came with us," Jeremy said awkwardly.

Sam must have seen the puzzled expression on Devon's face because he added, "Our moms are dating."

"Wait. What?" Devon said.

"Kids," Jeremy's mom called out. "Come sit down."

Sam traipsed over to the table. Jeremy started to follow, but Devon grabbed his arm.

"You never told me ..." Devon tilted her head. "Why didn't you tell me Sam was coming? And why have you never mentioned him before?"

Jeremy shrugged.

"You mentioned your mom was dating but I didn't realize it was so serious. Why didn't you … Oh ...You don't like your mom dating, do you?" Devon added sagely.

Jeremy's insides squirmed. He stayed silent and stared at a spot on the carpet.

"What if we have to do something for the TDC?" Devon continued.

"Travis must have known Sam was coming. Ends up he's the director of HR for Tech." Jeremy weaved through people settling down at large, round tables. "Did you get a note on the plane?"

"Yes," Devon said. "Maybe Travis will have a plan at the meeting."

5. The Assignment

Before they reached their table, Thing poked him in the side of the leg.

"What?" Jeremy whispered. Thing, swinging slightly, was red. Jeremy spotted a small, stuffed, red horse clipped to the bag of a girl about their age with short-cropped hair and glasses. He tapped Devon on the back, tilting his head toward the girl.

Devon raised her eyebrows before continuing to her seat, next to her parents. There was an empty chair between Devon and Sam, which Jeremy took. Devon leaned over and whispered, "Do you think—?"

"Check out Birdbrain and Thing," Jeremy interrupted. They were both red, a sign another detective was nearby.

Devon checked out both magic buddies and nodded. At that moment the servers, in white jackets, entered the dining hall with trays of food.

Five courses and two desserts later, Devon whispered to Jeremy, "Oh, it's seven twenty-five."

"Mom, I have to use the bathroom," Jeremy said.

"Okay."

"Me too," Devon said.

Someone started making a speech as Devon and Jeremy made their way toward the restrooms, which they passed, exiting the restaurant. They turned right and followed signs directing them to a stairwell.

Sam called out from behind. "Hey guys, wait up. Where are you going?"

Jeremy bristled. "I haven't seen Devon in a long time and wanted to catch up with her." His tone was dismissive.

Sam stopped in his tracks. "Oh."

"Jeremy," Devon whispered, "that's totally rude."

"Sam, it's okay," Devon called out. "We heard there was an observation deck upstairs and wanted to check it out. Don't really want to hang around for a bunch of speeches."

"Me neither, but..." Sam appeared to swallow his words.

Jeremy suddenly felt warm and stared down at his feet for a second.

"Jeremy!" Devon hissed.

Jeremy pulled his head up, focusing on a spot behind Sam's left shoulder. "Sorry, Sam," he mumbled. "Come on."

Sam followed them up the steps.

Three floors later, they pushed through a set of doors and walked outside onto the open-air deck of the fifty-ninth floor. Greeting them, the city of Paris glowed as if millions of stars had dropped down from the sky. The Eiffel Tower, taller than the other buildings by far and lit with thousands of lights, stood out like a beacon in the night.

"Dang, that's some view." Sam wandered off to get a better vantage point.

Devon's face lit up. "Oh wow, the Eiffel Tower."

"We were just there today." Jeremy searched for Travis. There were approximately thirty people on the platform, most at the edge, peering out at the city through a glass partition.

"I'm jealous. I can't wait to go."

Travis stood just ahead and off to their left, looking out at the city. Jeremy tapped Devon on the shoulder and headed toward Travis. Luckily, Sam stood a ways away, his back to them.

Just as Jeremy and Devon finished saying hi to Travis, the girl with the magic buddy walked up.

"Addison," Travis said. "This is Devon and Jeremy. Devon and Jeremy, this is Addison."

"Hey, what about us?" Thing called out, bouncing off Jeremy's leg.

"Yeah, don't forget us," Birdbrain said indignantly.

"Whoa, she's changed," Jeremy remarked to Devon.

"You could say that," Devon said.

"What's that supposed to mean?" Birdbrain said before pecking Devon on the leg.

"Just that in Portugal, because you were afraid of heights," Devon explained, "you were so quiet, but now—"

"You don't have to tell the whole world!" Birdbrain flapped her wings.

"Ahem." Travis raised his eyebrows. "As I was saying, this is Addison."

"No, Addie ... Call me Addie."

"Hi. Nice to meet you," Devon said. "I like your skirt."

Addie winced and looked at the ground. "Thanks," she mumbled.

"Yeah. Hi," Jeremy said.

"I'll get right to the point," Travis said. "We've been monitoring sites around the globe for signs of activity from extremist groups who want to use magic to increase their power, possibly take control of governments. Three to four weeks ago, we found evidence of a scheme to cause considerable panic here in Paris.

"When these two were in Portugal last year," he turned to Addie, "they found four magical objects that brought a statue to life. They flew with the statue to Pena Palace, where they restored the palace's colors. Someone removed the stones and medallions from the statue after they left."

Devon's jaw dropped. "How did they—?"

"What?" Jeremy said. The stones and medallions were embedded in the statue. Jeremy hadn't thought of taking them out. Having flown above the clouds on a statue that could talk had been enough to think about.

"We don't understand how he or she managed—" Travis said.

"It was that lady!" Jeremy exclaimed.

"What lady?" Addie asked in a heavy French accent.

"There was a woman who tried to trick—" Jeremy started.

Travis held up his hand. "We don't know who it was for sure, though that wouldn't surprise me. The important thing is, it happened. Then, about a month ago, we discovered the crushed man under a column at the reliquary of Saint Thomas Aquinas in Toulouse had vanished."

Addie gasped, putting a hand to her mouth. "No. What? That cannot be? How can he vanish? It is a fairy tale."

"Wait, what? Who is…? How is a man crushed under a column?" Jeremy stammered. While he'd had Thing for a year, the fact that magic existed in the world still took him by surprise each time something magical happened that wasn't related to Thing.

Devon seemed too shocked to say anything.

"There is what appears to be a crushed man under a column at the reliquary of Saint Thomas Aquinas," Travis explained. "Only his hands and feet are visible. There is a fairy tale about him, which Addie will read…. You brought the book?"

"Oui." Addie appeared dazed.

Travis continued. "We think someone used the stones and medallions to bring the crushed man back to life."

"So it is not just a story?" Addie was pulling at her shirt, untucking it from her flowered skirt.

"No, it's not."

Travis must have seen the puzzled expression on Jeremy's face. "Two stones and two medallions, each placed in a hand or foot. Your job is to figure out who did it and stop them. Our intelligence suggests there is a plan to take over the country, and possibly all of Europe. We are worried they will use magic to cause pandemonium by stealing objects, symbols of Paris.

"You need to stop them before they steal all that is important to this city and cause panic. We believe they want Paris to descend into chaos, and if it does, it would not only bring the city to a halt, it could disrupt the country, even the entire European Union. There could be financial meltdowns, accusations of interference between countries...."

"Who are these people?" Jeremy said.

"They're right-wing extremists. Members of a hate group who are fighting immigration and oppose people of color in positions of power."

"Doesn't matter if we're in power does it? Don't right-wing extremists just hate us because we're black?" Jeremy asked

Travis.

Travis nodded. "Yes, they do, Jeremy."

Jeremy and Travis stared at each other briefly before Travis continued. "Things have started to disappear."

"Why does everyone say—" Thing started.

Jeremy put his hand over where Thing's mouth would be.

"That doesn't stop me from talking, you know," Thing said.

"Shush." Jeremy removed his hand.

"Don't shush—"

"Cut it out!" Travis demanded, crossing his arms, his eyes narrowing. "This is not a game."

6. The Fairytale

"What has disappeared?" Addie asked.

Travis sighed, uncrossed his arms and placed them on his hips. "Someone stole a Monet from the Musée d'Orsay last night. The next target will most likely be bigger."

"Surely not le Louvre," Addie's eyes grew wider.

"Security is extremely tight, and they would have great difficulty, but I believe that is their next target."

"So someone is trying to steal works of art in order to cause chaos? That doesn't make sense," Jeremy said.

"Not just art, Jeremy," Travis said. "Stealing art may just be the beginning. Think what might happen if they start stealing landmarks."

"What?" Devon cried out. "How could they—?"

"They can use magic. So I think we should assume that anything is possible." Travis paused briefly. "This took us by surprise, actually. We thought the woman who pretended to be from the TDC wanted the stones to … take away the color from the Golden Gate Bridge."

Travis's pause was a little too long, as if he was choosing his words carefully.

"Yeah, I remember you saying that last summer," Devon said.

"But once someone stole the man from Saint Aquinas's reliquary, that suggested a much larger scheme."

"What are you doing about this?" Jeremy asked.

"You're not leaving it all up to us are you?" Devon said.

Travis was quiet for a moment. "We're working on other leads on this case. But you're the only ones who can use magic, which is why we need your help."

"Who's we?" Jeremy asked.

Travis ignored his question. "I have tickets to the Louvre for tomorrow that I will give to your parents," he said. "Start there. See what you can find."

"That's the plan?" Addie said. "We wander around the Louvre looking for what?"

"Um, Travis," Jeremy said, "I forgot to tell you.... Did you hear about our hotel room being broken into?"

"Yes, I did," said Travis.

"Well, I don't know if it's important, but someone stole the note stating the time and place of this meeting."

Travis stiffened and immediately scanned the area around them. "You should have told me sooner, Jeremy." Travis's voice was stern and landed like a reprimand.

"I'm sor—"

"I need to leave. There's a chance no one saw me with you," Travis said. "Addie, find somewhere to sit and read the story."

"What do we do about Sam?" Jeremy asked. Sam stood with his back to them, apparently engrossed in the view.

"That's the least of our worries," Travis said. "If you need to contact me, here's my number." He handed Devon a piece of paper and strode away.

"But—" Jeremy swallowed his words.

A man walked past, and as he did, he locked eyes with Jeremy before taking in the rest of the group.

"Um, that can't be good," Jeremy said.

Before Devon or Addie could respond, Sam walked up to them.

"What'cha all doin'? And what's with all the little kids' toys? You belong to a club or something?"

"Something like that," Jeremy replied snidely.

"Addie is sharing a story with us, a children's fairytale," Devon said after making introductions. "Not sure if it would interest you. But you're welcome to join us," she added, glaring at Jeremy.

"Nothing else to do." Sam said.

Addie, Devon and Jeremy walked to the side of the deck and sat down on the ground, leaning against the glass partition. Sam didn't sit, but stayed close by, facing out at the city. The number of people had grown since they came to meet Travis, but no one paid them any attention.

Addie pulled a book out of her camouflage shoulder bag, opened it and read silently for a moment before closing it. "If it is okay with you, I will just tell the story. It is too difficult to translate."

"Sure," Devon said, and Jeremy nodded.

Addie launched into a story about a greedy magician with magical powers who could make objects seemingly disappear by shrinking them until they fit in the palm of his hand. Friends and neighbors blamed one another when possessions went missing. But then they started accusing each other of the impossible: Stealing cows, trees, even crops. When an entire house vanished, people panicked.

The magician at the center of this story often drank too much, telling seemingly tall tales of finding great treasures. One night, he recounted a tale too familiar to the townspeople. He narrated the history of the town itself, of all that had disappeared, including crops and a house. When he spoke of a magician, he made the mistake of describing himself, right down to the hat on his head, which, he told them, granted the wearer any power he or she desired.

Sam joined them, sitting on the ground next to Jeremy. Addie carried on. The patrons in the bar coerced the magician into admitting that he shrank all the objects missing from the village. While admitting his role, the magician became childlike, cowering in the corner. They took the hat from him, and moments later, the magician turned to stone.

The Saint Thomas Aquinas reliquary was located in this town of Toulouse. Saint Thomas Aquinas wrote about the importance of virtues. He focused on the need to avoid four vices in particular: stealing, cowardice, poor judgment, and excessive drinking. And because the magician demonstrated all of these, the townspeople put him where he would be reminded of his mistakes. The column where they placed the magician is located behind the altar, within listening distance of Sunday sermons.

The town's residents magicked everything back to its original size. They then cut the hat four ways with each part transforming into a stone or metal medallion. Four men rode off on horseback, scattering the pieces in different directions. The fragments were never found again.

"That's a whopper," Sam said. "I've never heard that one before."

"Nope, me neither," added Devon.

They all sat quietly for a while.

"Maybe we should get back downstairs," Jeremy said. "Our parents are probably wondering where we are."

Once back in the restaurant, Jeremy searched for his mom, as people were no longer sitting at tables but standing around in groups. She and Cheryl were off to the side talking with Devon's parents. Jeremy tapped his mom on the shoulder. "Hi Mom."

"Hey, where've you been?" His mom sounded worried, and concern was etched on her face.

"Upstairs on the observation deck. It's really cool. You'd like it."

"What I'd like is for you to tell me when you're going somewhere." Her reprimand came through loud and clear.

Jeremy met his mom's gaze. "Sorry."

"It's okay, but next time do it differently, alright?" There was an edge to her voice. Jeremy nodded and repeated his apology.

His mom's gaze softened. "I'm still rattled from everything that happened today, and I was worried when I didn't know where you were."

Guilt bubbled up inside Jeremy, and he hunched, rounding his shoulders. He was usually good at letting his mom know where he was but he'd gotten caught up in meeting Travis and the fairy tale.

His mom continued. "Since we all have to work tomorrow, Cheryl has volunteered to explore the city with you kids."

"This is Addie." Jeremy motioned to Addie next to him. "Would it be okay if she joined us?"

"Making friends already." His mom smiled and introduced herself. "Sure. If it's all right with Cheryl."

"Sure," Cheryl said. "But why don't we check with your parents first, Addie."

Addie shoved her hands in the pockets of her skirt, and her gaze dropped to the floor. "Oh, they won't care."

Cheryl cocked her head to one side and gazed intently at Addie. "I'm sure they care."

Addie's body stiffened, and she smiled a little too suddenly as if covering for a mistake. "I was already planning to be on my own since they both have to work."

"I'd feel better if I met them first." Cheryl smiled quizzically.

Addie ran her hands through her short hair. "Okay. They're over there." She nodded toward a group of adults across the room. Tucking her shirt back into her skirt, she led Cheryl away.

7. The Louvre

Back at the apartment, Jeremy tapped his mom on the shoulder.

"Can I go hang out with Devon for a bit?"

"Jeremy, it's late."

"Please. For a few minutes?"

"If it's okay with her parents. But remember what we talked about before?" Her gaze drifted toward Sam.

Jeremy shifted uncomfortably, unsure how to respond.

"It's okay," Sam said, turning his back on Jeremy. "I'm tired anyway."

Ignoring his mom's reproving stare and his own internal

feeling of guilt, Jeremy slipped out of the room and knocked on the door down the hall.

Devon answered. "Oh, good. Mom said I could come out here for a few minutes before bed. Let's go down here." She pointed to the end of the hallway.

"Is your mom coming with us tomorrow?"

"No, she has a meeting, a videoconference." Devon sat down on the floor and leaned against the wall. "What do you think about that fairy tale?"

"What are we going to do about Sam?" Jeremy countered.

"You don't like him, do you?" said Devon.

"It's not that."

"What?"

"It's weird."

"What's weird?"

"My mom dating. I told her I was okay with it but I don't think I am. It's always been just the two of us."

"Well, try not to take it out on Sam. It's not his fault. You guys are kind of in the same situation."

"I guess." Jeremy paused. "But what are we going to do about him? He's not part of the TDC, and plus, he keeps making comments about our magic buddies." Jeremy peered down at Thing.

"Oh, hi there. Decided to remember me, huh." Thing bounced off Jeremy's leg.

"What are you going on about?" Jeremy asked.

"Here you two are yapping away, and you haven't even let me spend time with Birdbrain."

"Oh." said Devon "You're right."

"Of course I'm right."

Devon chuckled, unclipped Birdbrain and set her down at her side. Jeremy handed Thing over and Devon placed him next to her. Birdbrain flapped her wings and allowed Thing to hug her.

"Aww," said Jeremy.

Thing pointed at Jeremy. "Don't say a word."

Jeremy threw his hands up to shoulder height. "Wouldn't dream of it."

While the buddies hung out, Jeremy continued his conversation with Devon. "So, the fairy tale."

"Yeah. Where do we even start?"

"First, we have to figure out who it is," Jeremy said.

"And why they're doing it," Devon added.

"And how we're going to help," chimed Birdbrain.

"Yeah, you're going to need us," added Thing.

"It has to be that woman from Portugal, doesn't it?" Jeremy said.

"That seems to make the most sense. But why does she want to shrink things?"

"What? Someone wants to shrink me?" Thing exclaimed.

"No ... Thing ... I ..." Devon stammered.

"Ignore him, Devon. It's this new game he likes to play."

"Ffftttt," Thing exclaimed.

"Yeah, same to you," Jeremy said. Addressing Devon, he continued. "Maybe there's stuff she wants to steal, and this is how she can do it."

"Well, she's going to a lot of trouble," said Devon. "First trying to steal them from us, then figuring out how to take them out of the statue. Hmmm."

"What?"

"Why was she so intent on stealing them from us, when she could just take them out of the statue?"

"No idea," said Jeremy.

"Well, at least you're consistent." Thing patted Jeremy on the leg and winked at Birdbrain.

***

The next day Jeremy, Sam, Devon and Cheryl met Addie outside the Louvre. It was a beautiful summer morning without a cloud in the sky. The morning chill gone, Jeremy was glad he'd chosen to leave his jacket behind. Crowds of tourists congregated outside in the open plaza, some huddled in groups, some sitting on the concrete edge of one of several fountains. Others lined up to enter the Louvre via the large pyramid. Made of glass and metal, six stories tall, it towered over the square and served as an entrance to the museum.

"Hi, Addie," Devon said. "Are you okay?"

This question surprised Jeremy. He hadn't noticed at first, but Addie's eyes were red.

"Yes." Addie seemed to force a smile while fingering a buckle on the camouflage bag strapped across her chest.

As they stood in a circle, Sam asked for the third time, "Mom, why are we going here?"

"Sam, I told you. This is one of the most, if not the most, famous museum in the world, and it wouldn't hurt you to have a cultural experience. Besides, I've always wanted to go. And Mr. Davis got us tickets."

Devon couldn't contain her excitement, bouncing up and down on her toes. "I've wanted to come here for ages."

"Well, do you know what you want to see?" asked Addie. "Because you could spend weeks here and not see everything."

"The Mona Lisa for sure," said Cheryl.

"The Venus de Milo," added Devon.

Both Jeremy and Sam gaped at Devon. "What?"

"It's a statue of Venus … or Aphrodite." The others stared at her, so she continued. "The goddess of love and beauty."

Addie's shoulders were rounded, her hands in the pockets of her cargo shorts. "What you don't want to do is wander around aimlessly, because you might miss what's important to you."

Cheryl pointed toward the entrance at the pyramid. "Well, let's get a map and pick a few things."

Jeremy groaned at Cheryl's word choice.

"Not this entrance." Addie steered them away from the growing crowds. "There's another one that will be quicker."

While Addie steered them past the glass pyramid to an underground entrance, Thing grumbled.

"Oh, here we go," Jeremy said to Devon.

"No respect," said Thing. "That's what I say. No respect."

Devon chuckled and held the door open for Jeremy.

They passed a relatively small inverted glass pyramid and joined a line that was one third the length of the outside queue. After they handed in their tickets, Addie made a suggestion. "Let's go to the Mona Lisa first, yes? It's less crowded in the morning."

"What's the big deal about the Mona Lisa?" Sam asked as they started off.

"Well, Leonardo da Vinci painted it, and he's really famous," Jeremy said. "Some guy, Francesco de something, I forgot his last name, hired da Vinci. He wanted the painting to thank his wife for having his two children. Though actually, I think that's just one theory. I don't think anyone really knows."

At this point everyone stopped and looked at Jeremy, causing several people to almost bump into them. They passed by, muttering disapproval in various languages.

"Let me guess." Devon's eyes twinkled. "You did some research last night."

"Of course." Jeremy grinned.

"Okay." Devon smiled. "Go on. Why is this particular painting famous?"

"Because it was stolen in 1910 or 1911," Jeremy said.

"So?" Sam started walking down the hallway and the others followed.

"So, that's why it's famous. An employee of the museum stole the Mona Lisa and kept it in his apartment for a couple of years. The employee was Italian and so was Leonardo, and the employee believed the Mona Lisa should be in an Italian museum. When he tried to sell the painting to a museum in Italy, he was caught."

"But why is it famous?" Sam asked.

"Oh, I remember something about this," Devon said. "The fact that it was stolen made it famous."

Jeremy nodded. "He also used some special painting technique where he painted one layer at a time and then waited for it to dry before painting the next one. It took him, like, three years to finish."

Signs indicated that the Mona Lisa was on the first floor, and they passed French paintings from 1780-1850 on their way.

"It really does have its own room," Sam said.

With the museum just opening, they were among the first ones there. Jeremy stepped up to the painting. He only had time to take a first look, before an alarm sounded in the main hall.

Jeremy froze.

Addie stepped toward the sound. "Come on," she insisted.

Devon and Jeremy turned and raced with her out of the room into the main hallway leaving Sam and Cheryl behind.

"Wait!" Cheryl called out, but Jeremy continued with the others.

Following the sound of the alarm, they ran downstairs to the ground floor and came upon a crowd of people, including several members of security shouting into their radios.

"Oh no." Devon opened her map of the museum.

"What?" Jeremy glanced over Devon's shoulder at the map.

"Oh no, no, no," Devon said, louder. "It's gone."

"What's gone?"

"The Venus de Milo."

"You never said if she was Venus or Aphrodite," Birdbrain called from Devon's side.

"Both." Devon rubbed her neck. "She's the goddess of love but the Greeks and Romans called her by different names."

"You humans are so weird," Birdbrain remarked.

Meanwhile, the surrounding room was in chaos. Guards shouted and ran around, while more visitors wandered to the area, drawn by the commotion.

"How can it disappear?" Addie appeared momentarily frozen, her eyes staring at the space once occupied by the statue.

"The man from St. Thomas Aqu—" Devon's voice trembled slightly.

"I know, I know," Addie interrupted, coming out of her trance. "I didn't really believe Mr. Davis until now."

Jeremy searched the people around them. "Devon, look for the woman from Portugal."

"What does she look like?" Addie said.

Devon was twirling her hair. "I don't see—"

A second alarm punctuated the air.

Jeremy spun toward the sound. "Another one?"

Without a word, Addie started running. She led Jeremy and Devon back the way they'd come, until they ran into Cheryl and Sam in a corridor being questioned by security.

8. The Man From Portugal

The hallway was in chaos. Voices and crackles blared from radios, several security guards were running in different directions. Others were trying to contain visitors attracted by the commotion.

"What's going on?" Jeremy asked Sam, who hovered off to the side, while his mom talked to security.

"I don't know." Sam's eyes kept darting to his mom. "Mom kept me from running after you, but while we were arguing about what to do next, an alarm sounded inside the room, and two men left. We looked, and the Mona Lisa was gone."

"Two men? Are you sure about that?"

"Yeah, why?"

"Nothing." Jeremy moved alongside Devon who was leaning against a wall.

"Sam says two men left right after the alarm sounded."

"That doesn't make sense," Devon said. "Did he give you a description?"

"I didn't ask." Jeremy walked back to Sam.

"What did the men look like?" Jeremy asked.

"I'm not sure … didn't really see them. Pretty average looking. One was yay high." Sam held his hand several inches above his head. "The other was about my height. That man must have been really old cuz his skin was pasty, and he walked all stiff like. The other, taller one was just a normal guy."

"What do you mean by normal?" Jeremy thought he knew what Sam meant.

"You know, normal," Sam said.

"No, I don't know," Jeremy snapped. "You mean like white normal?" He was surprised at how quickly he was getting angry.

"Well, yeah."

Jeremy scrunched his eyes, and stared at Sam.

"Oh crap, Jeremy, I'm—"

Before Sam could finish, Jeremy strode away.

"Hey, what's the matter?" Devon caught up with Jeremy.

"Sam's the matter, that's what," Jeremy scowled.

"What happened?" Devon asked.

"Nothing." Jeremy closed his eyes and sighed, shaking his head.

"Really? Nothing?" said Thing.

"Shut it."

"Hey, don't take it out on me." Thing kicked Jeremy's leg.

Devon was watching him. Jeremy clenched his teeth.

"Why is it that whenever someone breaks the law and they're black, everyone is quick to point out that the black guy did it. But when it's some white dude, they say he was a normal guy or don't mention the fact that he was white?"

"Is that what happened with Sam?" Devon asked.

"Yeah, and I'm ticked off," Jeremy said.

Sam shuffled forward with his head down. "I'm sorry." He jabbed at the floor with his shoe.

"Do you even know what you're sorry for?" Jeremy practically shouted. Without waiting for an answer, he turned away. "Just leave me alone." He trudged into an adjoining room and stared absentmindedly at a painting, not noticing that Cheryl had joined him until she spoke.

"Hey, I heard what happened between you and Sam. Sam said he apologized, but I understand that you're still mad."

"I don't want to talk about it, okay." Jeremy stepped to the next painting.

"I just want to—"

Jeremy cut her off. "I don't have to talk to you. You're not my mother!" Jeremy stormed out of the room.

"Hey, where are you going?" Devon stepped toward him as he filed past. "Shouldn't we be searching for—?"

"I need some space." He passed her without making eye contact. Not paying attention to where he was going, Jeremy became lost in the labyrinth that was the Louvre. In his haste to find his way, he swung around too quickly and bumped into a man coming out of a bathroom.

"Sorry," Jeremy mumbled, catching just a glimpse of the man's face before continuing on. The guy looked vaguely familiar, but Jeremy was too preoccupied to give it a second thought. Thing kicked him in the side. Thing was blue, meaning a clue was nearby, but this didn't register with Jeremy. Ten minutes later, having finally made it outside, he found a spot on some stairs and sat watching the crowd and trying to calm his tumultuous thoughts.

"You okay?" Thing asked quietly from his side.

Jeremy regarded him for a moment before speaking. "Yeah…. I mean, no I'm really mad right now, but I'll get over it."

Devon came up from behind and sat next to him. "It might help if you talk about it."

"Hey," Jeremy met her gaze briefly. "Maybe, but I'm not really up for that now, if you don't mind." His tone was sharper than he intended.

"Sure, but don't bark at me."

Jeremy smiled despite his anger. "Bark?"

"Oh, I don't know, it just slipped out. But really, I'd rather you didn't take your anger out on me. And perhaps you can go easier on Sam. He's not responsible for a world's worth of racial profiling."

"Yeah, I know."

Addie sat down next to Devon. "Why are you out here? We should be inside trying to figure out what happened."

"It was getting too crazy in there. Besides, I don't think whoever stole the art is going to hang around." Devon said. "Did you see Sam or his mom?"

"Yes, Sam's mom said they had to stay inside and talk to security and asked that we wait for them out here."

"Perfect." Devon started twirling her hair. "That gives us some time to talk. Did you hear Sam say he saw two men leaving?"

"Yes, but that does not make sense, no? I thought we were looking for a woman."

"That's what we thought too," Devon replied. "It doesn't make any sense."

Jeremy swung around with a start, staring at Devon while shaking his finger. "Yes, it does."

"How?"

"There was someone else trying to get the stones in Portugal, remember? He confronted us at the park and then chased after us but we flew away."

"What do you mean, flew away?" Addie asked.

"Oooooohhhhh, it was amazing!" Birdbrain pushed away from Devon's side and flapped her wings.

"Shhh," Devon admonished. "When we were in Portugal, we found two stones and two medallions, and when we put them in the statue of King John, he came to life, and we flew with him to Pena Palace."

"And … it … was … awesome!" Birdbrain flapped her wings, hovering briefly at Devon's waist.

"Yeah, it was," Thing added with a backflip.

"Can you all stop!" Jeremy rested his head in his hands, covering his eyes. His frustration with Sam, and his fear about his mom dating, combined with the events in the museum, were overwhelming him.

"Cranky." The sound of Birdbrain flapping her wings ceased.

Jeremy sat up. Devon was watching him, chin resting on her hand. He took a deep breath. "Remember that guy who chased us?"

"Yeah." Devon sat up. "Why?"

"Before I left the museum, I bumped into someone, and ever since something has been bothering me. I realize now that he looked familiar. It's the same guy."

"Are you sure?" Devon resumed twirling her hair.

"Yes, I'm sure. And … wait … Thing turned blue, and … that's why you kicked me." He peered down at Thing.

"Well, you didn't seem to be paying attention."

Jeremy stared at Thing for a moment. "We saw the guy up close at the park, remember." He raised his head and eyed Devon. "Plus, he must have a skimpy wardrobe, cuz he was wearing the same shirt, the one with the diagonal stripe on it, that he was wearing in Portugal."

"So a man that ran after you in Portugal stole the stones and medallions and now is here?" Addie's gaze shifted between Jeremy and Devon. "But why?

"Because it is fun," called out a new voice near Addie, who peered at the magic buddy clipped to her bag.

"What?" Addie asked.

"Because … it … is … fun," repeated the horse, enunciating each syllable snootily, suggesting that it had never had fun in its life.

"That's not a good reason." Addie scrunched her eyes.

"You humans do things for the most absurd reasons." The horse flicked his tail.

"Besides," Devon chimed in, "Travis mentioned something about causing—"

Thing interrupted, his eyes wide. "Did you say, 'do things?'"

"Not now," Jeremy said.

"Oh, it's ok for you to go off in a huff but—"

"Sometimes I wish you had a mouth," Jeremy said, "so I could cover it with my hand."

"Ffftttt!"

"Whose mouth do you want to … wait, who doesn't have a mouth?" Sam sidled up beside Devon.

"Nothing," Jeremy said. "Just an inside joke."

"Oh." Sam's forced smile faded.

Devon stood up to greet Sam. "See anything interesting?"

"Nah, though my mom did."

Sam was eyeing Jeremy. Jeremy's shoulders slumped, and he averted his gaze.

"Where is she?" Devon asked.

"She's coming." Sam glanced at the museum and nodded. "There she is."

"Everything all right out here?" Cheryl was clearly addressing Jeremy.

"Yeah." Jeremy eyed the ground.

"Anybody hungry?" Cheryl asked.

"Yes," everyone said in unison.

"Ok then, let's find some food. Perhaps, Addie, you have some suggestions?"

9. Struggle

Later that night, lying in bed, Jeremy went over the events of the day. Frustrated by an inability to figure out what to do about their assignment, his mind drifted to what he realized was resentment of Sam and Cheryl as well as his own mom who had cornered him after dinner.

"Jeremy, I heard you had some words with Sam," his mom said.

"Yeah," he said, his eyes fixed on a spider climbing the wall.

"Can you please try—"

Jeremy faced his mom. "He was being racist!"

"I don't think—"

"Not you too!" Jeremy stared at his mom.

"What?" She tilted her head, her eyes searching his.

"Never mind." He turned away.

"Jeremy." She almost whispered his name, touching him gently on the shoulder.

"What?" His shoulders sagged.

"Will you let me finish?"

Jeremy didn't answer, but turned back to face his mom.

"What I was going to say was that I don't think your anger with Sam is entirely due to what he said."

Jeremy looked away from his mom.

"No, listen. Could he be more aware of what he's saying? Sure. Has he grown up in the US where being white is considered normal," she held up her hands and signed quotation marks, "and bias is everywhere? Sure. But that's not what this is about. You say you're fine with me seeing Cheryl, but I'm not so sure. Might you be taking out your feelings on Sam instead of me?"

"I don't want to talk about it," he said and walked away.

But now, lying in bed, he had to admit she was right. He wasn't okay with it. Sam wasn't half bad, but he wished both he and his mom would go away. Scowling, he said to himself, "I just want things to go back to normal."

"You mean like white normal?" Thing whispered from the edge of the bed.

"Very funny," Jeremy replied and rolled over onto his side, away from Thing.

***

The following morning, Jeremy's mom made an announcement at breakfast. "Cheryl and I talked, and we agreed that perhaps we need to change plans for today. I spoke last night with Mr. Davis and he assures me that Addie can show you and Devon around the city today, and Cheryl and Sam are going to have time for themselves."

Heat coursed through Jeremy's body and he was conscious of his face burning. "I'm sorry about taking things out on Sam yesterday."

"He's sitting right there," Jeremy's mom said.

Jeremy took a deep breath and faced Sam. "I'm sorry for snapping at you yesterday. You didn't deserve it…. Though you do have a lot to learn," he added.

Jeremy's mom cleared her throat.

"What? It's true," Jeremy said.

"While it may be true—" his mom started to say.

"It's okay," Sam interjected. "He's right. I'm sorry for what I said. But it's also not my fault that our moms are dating," he said, locking eyes with Jeremy.

Jeremy broke eye contact and fiddled with his eggs, picking them up with his fork and flipping them back over onto the plate.

"What would help you, Jeremy?" Cheryl said kindly.

Jeremy shrugged, continuing to play with his eggs.

"You are still the most important person in your mom's life. I will never try to come between you two. You know that, right?"

Jeremy nodded without looking up before pulling his attention away from his plate and toward Sam. "It's okay if you want to come with us today, Sam."

"Thanks, Jeremy," Cheryl said. "But I want to have some time just with Sam. The decision to change plans today wasn't only because of what happened yesterday. Sam and I also need to have time just for us."

Jeremy locked eyes with Sam and unfurrowed his brow. "Okay. So maybe tomorrow we can hang?"

"Sure," Sam grinned. "Just don't go to the Arc de Triomphe today, okay. I want to see that with you tomorrow."

"Okay." Jeremy allowed himself to smile.

***

"Where's Sam?" Devon asked, when Jeremy met up with her in the hallway and started off toward the elevator.

"He's spending the day with his mom." Jeremy filled her in on the morning's conversation.

"Where should we go?" Devon asked.

"Not sure. Let's see if Addie has any ideas."

Addie was waiting for them outside the doors of the hotel.

"Why does she look like a boy?" Thing said.

"What do you mean, look like a boy?" Devon asked. "Do only boys get to wear hats and shorts?"

"Never mind," Thing said.

"Why don't you look like something other than a blob?" Birdbrain teased while flapping her wings.

"Oh, I'm going to get you," Thing said, straining at the end of his carabiner as Jeremy opened the door and stepped outside into the warm morning air.

"Ready to go?" Addie asked.

"Yep," replied Jeremy, laughing at Birdbrain and Thing. "But we can't go to the Arc de Triomphe today."

"Oh?" Addie raised her eyebrows.

"Blob," Birdbrain said, taunting Thing.

"Sam asked that we wait until tomorrow to see it. He's off somewhere with his mom today but wants to hang with us tomorrow."

"Hang?" Addie asked, a puzzled expression on her face.

"Be with us," Devon interjected.

"Oh. I thought you wanted to climb a tree." Addie adjusted her hat. "You have such crazy expressions."

Jeremy doubled over laughing. "Okay … no … okay … sorry … What?" he added, eyeing Devon. "It was funny … climb a tree." Shaking his head, Jeremy attempted to stifle his laughter.

Jeremy, Devon and Addie meandered away from the hotel, crossing a busy street with the light. Another beautiful, warm morning, Jeremy wished he had worn shorts too. Having recovered his composure enough to ask a question, Jeremy spoke up. "Do we have any idea how to find these guys?"

"Well, the one man seems to like art." Devon said.

They ambled single file down the sidewalk, avoiding people hurrying to work in the opposite direction.

"But we still don't know why he's choosing to steal art," Jeremy said. Devon and Addie stopped and stood off to the side, and Jeremy edged up next to them. "What if that's only the beginning? If only we could find a pattern."

"Horsey over there said it was because it's fun," Thing offered in a tone that suggested it was the stupidest idea ever.

"Blob," Birdbrain teased.

"I'm warning you," Thing said.

"Or what?" Birdbrain said.

"Do not call me Horsey," the horse interjected, standing erect with his head held high. "My name is Napoleon."

Thing launched a backflip off Jeremy's leg. "Well, congratulations."

"What is your name?" Napoleon asked.

"Never you mind," Thing said curtly.

"I think your name is not nearly as grand as mine." Napoleon shook his mane before swishing his tail.

"Oh, it's not," Birdbrain chuckled.

"Are you guys done?" Jeremy asked.

"No," Thing said.

"Well, cut it out for now, will you. We've got a lot to figure out."

Jeremy caught sight of Thing staring down Birdbrain as the group continued down the street.

10. The Sacré-Cœur

"We have to stop here," Addie said, standing in front of a bakery whose name Jeremy couldn't pronounce. "It is the best pâtisserie in this part of the city." She led the way into a small shop whose shelves were filled with large puffed pastries, small cakes, croissants, turnovers, and tarts.

"Do all bakeries in Paris smell this good?" Jeremy asked no one in particular.

After paying for their croissants, turnovers and éclairs, they headed for the exit.

"What if," Devon stopped before they reached the door, "Napoleon is partially right. No wait," she said in response to

Thing rolling his eyes. "What if one of the reasons this guy from Portugal wants to steal art pieces … well, not because it's fun, but because he wants them for his own personal collection?"

The bakery was crowded with Parisians and tourists ordering pastries, so the group stepped outside onto the still busy sidewalk and stood against the side of the building.

"That still doesn't narrow down what he's planning to steal next," Jeremy said. "And what if he starts to go after more than art? The fairy tale mentioned whole houses disappearing…. And Travis seemed to think someone was trying to take down governments, not steal art for a personal collection."

"True, but if stealing art is his way of doing that, we could consider what he might go for next. Unless you have a better idea?" Devon added.

Jeremy shook his head.

"Any suggestions?" Devon asked Addie. She paused before adding, "Addie. Are you alright?"

Addie appeared to be lost in thought and her eyes glistened.

"What?" Addie stammered. "Yes."

"What's wrong?" Devon said.

Addie stood with her gaze averted, apparently trying to hold back tears.

"What's going on?" Jeremy asked. "Is it something at home?"

Addie sighed and looked up, wiping her eyes. "My parents and I got into an argument this morning. They don't like how I dress, or how I have my hair."

Addie was wearing gray shorts and a plain black t-shirt. Red tennis shoes and a black beanie hat bookended her wardrobe.

"What's wrong with what you're wearing?" Jeremy asked.

"They think I should wear clothes that are more feminine, that I should have my hair long ..." Addie fixed her gaze on the ground. "They're worried that I'm gay."

"Oh, Addie," Devon said, "that must be so hard."

Addie looked at Devon with appreciation.

"I was worried that if I told you, you would not want to be with me."

"Why wouldn't we want to be with you?" Devon asked.

"Yeah, why? You do know my mom and Sam's mom are dating, right?" Jeremy said.

"I wondered …" Addie's voice trailed off, but her eyes were no longer scrunched and her body visibly relaxed. Taking a deep breath, Addie smiled for the first time that morning. "Thank you. It helps just to have someone else know."

"Of course," Devon said. "If you need to talk, we're here."

"Yeah," Jeremy seconded.

"Thanks."

They turned and started down the still bustling street. "How about we figure out which museum to go to …" Addie's voice trailed off when they walked past a newspaper stand. "Oh no!"

"What?" Devon and Jeremy asked.

Addie grabbed a paper from a stack. "They have closed all the museums."

"What?" Jeremy and Devon chorused.

"They have closed all the museums ... because of the thefts."

Stunned, they stood in silence, until passersby bumped into them, shaking them out of their reverie.

"What now? I don't suppose he'll just stop," Jeremy said.

"If he is really interested in art, he may go to Montmartre," Addie said.

"What is—?" Jeremy started.

"Oh, the artist's village, right?" Devon said. "And the Sacré-Cœur. It's supposed to be beautiful!"

Jeremy stared at Devon. How'd she know all this?

"I've always wanted to go to Paris, all right. I've done my research," she ended defensively.

"At least my person has done her research," Birdbrain said to Thing.

"I know. My guy is hopeless. No need to remind me." Thing bounced off Jeremy's leg.

"Hey!" Jeremy said.

"You Americans are very funny," Addie said. "Let's go to le Montmartre, at least until we come up with another idea."

"Yes, they are silly," added Napoleon.

"Oh, I don't like that guy," Thing muttered, so only Jeremy could hear. Thing continued his rant, and Jeremy caught the words "horsey" and "snobbish."

Emerging from the train at the Abbesses station, they headed toward the stairs.

"Oh wow," said Devon breathlessly. "It's so beautiful."

Jeremy followed her gaze to the wall lining the stairwell, and he understood what she meant. A mural representing the city of Paris spread out along the entire wall in vivid colors of yellow, purple, green and red. The sun appeared to be shining down on the Eiffel Tower.

"You like it?" Addie asked Devon.

"I love it. I've never seen anything like it."

"Would you like to see more?"

"There's more of them?" Devon asked.

"Yes. Many more. I come here a lot just to see the murals."

Distracted from the group's objective, Addie meandered through the station, showing off the many colorful walls, including one that had the Sacré-Cœur itself. "I have one more to show you. This is Napoleon's favorite."

"Oh really. The horsey likes art, does he," Thing said.

"Don't be so rude, Thing," Jeremy scolded.

"What did you call him?" Napoleon asked.

"Never you mind," Thing said.

"I thought I heard you say …" but Napoleon didn't finish, distracted by the stairwell in front of them. "Oh, it is so beautiful, no?" He was staring transfixed at the mural, the background of which was in multiple shades of blue, overlaid with white flying horses with bushy tails. "Oh, how I would love to fly," he said.

"Yes, perhaps you could sprout wings and fly away," Thing muttered to himself.

"What is it with you?" Jeremy whispered to Thing. "Why don't you like Napoleon? Wait, are you jealous?"

"Jealous … me? … No … Why would I be jealous?" Thing stammered.

"Cuz he's a horse with an impressive name and you're—"

"...want to fly too," Birdbrain was saying.

"Why does everyone want to fly? What's so cool about that?" Thing said.

"Who's mister grouchy over there?" Birdbrain said.

"If you don't want to fly, what would you want to do?" Napoleon asked.

They all stared at Thing.

"What do you mean what would I want to do? If I could have another magical power?" Napoleon nodded. "I have some ideas but …" Thing glanced up at Jeremy. "I'll keep them to myself for now."

"Why?" Jeremy asked.

"You might not approve."

Jeremy chuckled. "Like you feel you need my approval. You certainly didn't need my approval when you put Cheerios in my bed sheets last month."

"He didn't," Devon said.

"Oh, yes I did," Thing said.

Addie stepped in. "We need to be going now, yes?"

They exited the station into the bright sunshine and wandered toward an open air market. Jeremy briefly stumbled on the cobblestone boulevard. Artists painted on easels and displayed their portraits of the Sacré-Cœur, the Eiffel Tower, even knock-offs of Monets, for the multitudes of tourists wandering around.

Up the street, they passed through an open plaza where children were playing soccer. Others rode a carousel off in the corner.

"Addie," Devon asked, "why is there a carousel here?"

"Why? I'm not sure. There are carousels all over the city. For the children I suppose. They are very fun, yes?"

"Yes, I—"

But at that moment an alarm sounded from the Sacré-Cœur. Several flights of stairs above them, people streamed out of the doors. Security personnel ushered the crowd down the hill.

"What are they saying?" Jeremy asked Addie as those who first exited the basilica made it down to their level.

"Something about a fire alarm," Addie replied.

Suddenly, in the blink of an eye, the Sacré-Cœur disappeared, and panicked cries erupted from the crowd.

"Oh no!" Devon cried. "We're too late."

Jeremy turned around in circles, scanning the crowd.

Addie started running away.

"Wait! Addie! Where are you going?" Jeremy called out after her. "Devon, come on."

11. Following and Followed

Screams punctuated the air around them. The Sacré-Cœur had disappeared. Jeremy couldn't believe it. He grabbed Devon's hand, pulling her, as he ran after Addie. They had to zigzag through people rushing in all directions. He stopped running when Addie climbed onto a brown horse attached to the carousel.

"Addie, I don't think it's the right time …" Jeremy didn't finish because his mouth dropped open. The horse on which Addie climbed broke free of the carousel and cantered toward them. It stopped in front of Jeremy and Devon who stood frozen, mouths agape.

"Climb on!" Addie cried.

They scrambled up, Devon behind Addie and Jeremy at the rear.

"Behold my new magical power!" gloated Napoleon.

With the eyes of the crowd still locked on the place where the Sacré-Cœur vanished, the horse took a running start and launched into the air.

"I wanted to fly myself, but I could not make myself bigger and fly for those are two powers. So I thought this was—," Napoleon said.

Addie interrupted. "Not now. Concentrate on where we're going."

They flew away from the crowd to avoid detection and then doubled back, scanning the crowd for the men they knew were responsible for the Sacré-Cœur's disappearance. Below them was a scene of complete chaos. People were screaming, some trying to run away from the area, while others from nearby streets were drawn to the site by all of the noise. It reminded Jeremy of vehicles at an intersection without a traffic signal, where everyone goes at the same time, and cars become stuck, blocked in from all sides.

"There!" cried Devon, pointing to her right. Two men were

running, one stiffly, away from the crowd.

"We need to get lower," Jeremy exclaimed.

Napoleon whinnied, and the horse they were riding started to descend.

They hit the pavement at a gallop, scattering people around them, but Addie pulled on the reins to slow down.

"We're losing them!" Jeremy stated.

"We cannot run through the crowd. People could get hurt," Addie said.

Jeremy jumped off the horse and took off at a sprint. Devon called out after him, but he ignored her. The men were ahead of him across an empty plaza. The taller one glanced over his shoulder then picked up his pace.

"Faster," Thing said. "I need you to get closer."

"What?" Jeremy said, gulping for air.

"Faster."

"I'm ... trying." By the time Jeremy got to the other side of the plaza, there was no sign of the men, but a piece of paper fluttered to the ground. Bending over, gasping for breath, he picked it up. Scrawled in barely legible writing was a list:

Musée d'Orsay Monet

Louvre Venus de Milo, Mona Lisa

Sacré-Cœur

Eiffel Tower

Arc de Triomphe

"Hey guys … look." Jeremy was still breathing hard when Devon and Addie caught up with him. "I think they're going for the Eiffel Tower next," he said, showing them the piece of paper.

"Must not be too bright if he has to carry a list around," Thing said.

"Those are some big things he wants to steal," Birdbrain chuckled, eyeing Thing.

"Hey!" Thing started. He pushed off from Jeremy's leg toward Birdbrain but was stopped short by the carabiner clip.

"Just kidding," Birdbrain said with a flap of her wings.

Sirens punctuated the air. Jeremy turned. A large crowd milled about at the base of the stairs leading up to the site of the vanished Sacré-Cœur.

"Jeremy, can I see that?" Addie asked.

Jeremy pulled his attention away from the crowd. Addie was holding out her hand, and he gave her the paper. When she turned it over, an insignia from a hotel decorated the top of the page. "The Hôtel Régyn's Montmartre is not too far from here," Addie said. "Let's go."

"What about the horse?" Napoleon asked. For a moment they all watched the horse eating flowers from in front of a nearby building. Curious onlookers were racing toward the growing crowd. The three of them stood still and unnoticed.

"We need to leave it here. Perhaps it can find its way back," Addie said.

"Leave her here? That is my magical comrade and you want me to leave her here?" Napoleon complained.

"Please, Napoleon. Perhaps you will see her later."

Napoleon hung his head in defeat. Addie started off, and Jeremy and Devon raced after her. The hotel came into view, just as two men hurried through the double doors.

Near the entrance, Addie stopped. "You two stay here. I will be right back."

"Wait, what?" Jeremy said, but Addie took off.

"Let her go." Devon grabbed Jeremy's arm to keep him from following. "She'll be inconspicuous on her own, especially since she's French."

"Okay, okay," Jeremy replied. He wasn't used to hanging back and waiting.

They sat down on a bench outside, while Birdbrain and

Thing entertained themselves by having a staring contest. Sirens still sounded in the distance. A helicopter flew overhead.

Jeremy stared at the ground. How were they going to get the Sacré-Cœur and the art work back? How could they stop these men from stealing more objects? Where was Addie?

"What's taking her so long?" Jeremy said. It had been nearly ten minutes since she'd gone inside.

"Be pa—oh, there she is," Devon said.

"They're in room 527," Addie stated, walking up to them.

"How do you—?" Jeremy started.

Addie cut him off. "I followed them," she replied. "And I got a key to their room." She held up a flat key card.

"How did you manage that?" Jeremy eyed her with a new appreciation.

"When I came back downstairs, I told them I was the man's daughter and asked if I could have a third key. Hotels are sometimes relaxed on these things."

"No one better relax on me!" Thing bounced off Jeremy's leg, but everyone ignored him.

"Okay, so now what?" Jeremy asked.

"We need to get into their room and search for the Sacré-

Cœur and the other pieces of art," Devon said.

"Devon, really. I didn't know you had it in you." Jeremy gaped at her.

"Do you have a better idea?" Devon asked.

"Well, no. And I didn't say it was a bad idea. I was just surprised to hear it from you, is all."

"There's one problem." Devon glanced at her watch. "It's getting late, and if we don't get back, my mom and dad won't let me go out on my own again."

"Good point," said Jeremy.

"Can you meet me tomorrow morning?" Addie asked.

"We'll figure out a way," Devon replied. "Can you help us find our way back to the hotel?"

"Yes."

"Can't we just take the horse?" asked Napoleon.

"I don't think we should draw attention to ourselves," Addie said. "Besides, the sight of it might be too much for Paris to handle after all that has happened."

Walking down the street toward the metro, the hairs on Jeremy's neck stood up, and his body broke out with goosebumps. He stopped and spun around, searching.

"What's wrong?" Devon said, turning to face the same

direction.

"I'm not sure. I just got the feeling we were being followed."

"Um, look at our buddies," Addie said uneasily.

As Jeremy glanced down at a now purple Thing, a van with darkened windows stopped in the middle of the road. Two men got out and headed toward them. Through the open door, a familiar face peered back at Jeremy.

Jeremy sensed danger, and he could tell by the expression on their faces that Devon and Addie felt the same.

"In here!" Addie called out and the three of them ran into a cafe to their right. The men turned around and returned to the van, not brazen enough to try anything with so many witnesses. Jeremy felt Devon shaking next to him. He was trembling too. Once they were sure the coast was clear, and the buddies were no longer purple, the three of them headed directly to the metro.

"What was that about?" Jeremy said. His adrenaline rush had not quite worn off.

Neither Devon nor Addie responded except to shake their heads.

"Devon, there was a third person in that van. It was her."

"Who?"

"The lady from Portugal."

Devon stopped. "No…. Are you sure?"

Jeremy halted mid stride and faced her. "Pretty sure … yeah."

Addie came back toward them. "Did I hear you say there is another person here from Portugal, and now she's after us?"

"It certainly seems like it," Jeremy said. They all stood quietly for a moment, lost in thought.

"We'd better get back to the hotel," Devon said.

Addie stayed with them on the metro, making sure they got off at the right stop. Jeremy and Devon walked to their hotel, and Jeremy kept looking over his shoulder. They didn't talk until they were safely inside.

12. Worry and Trust

On the ride up the elevator, Devon broached the subject of
Sam. "If Sam is going to be with us tomorrow, I don't know
how we can avoid telling him what we're up to."

"So ... what? We just spill the beans about the TDC?"
Jeremy asked as the elevator came to a stop on the fifth floor.

The doors opened, and they stepped out. "I think we'll have
to." Devon said. "Plus, maybe he'll be helpful."

"Right," Jeremy said testily.

Devon stopped in the middle of the hallway and faced
Jeremy. "Why do you have to be so hard on him? I get that
you feel threatened by Cheryl, but it's not Sam's fault."

"I don't feel—"

"Really?" accused Devon.

They stared at each other. Jeremy broke eye contact first, his gaze dropping to the floor.

"Ok," Jeremy said, wanting to deflect the conversation. "But what about our parents? We definitely can't do anything with them around. We can't just ditch Cheryl, and what about your mom?"

They took the remaining steps to Jeremy's hotel room.

"I'm guessing she's got work to do." Devon said.

"There you are!" Jeremy's mom enveloped him in a hug before he could walk through the door. For some reason Devon's parents were also in the suite. Devon's mom grabbed her too.

"Mom ... Mom ... you're squeezing me." Jeremy's mom let go of him. "What's going on?" Tension permeated the room. Sam was sitting in their bedroom with his head in his hands. "What's wrong with Sam?"

Tears were running down his mom's face. "Cheryl's been taken."

Jeremy's mind went blank. "Taken?... What do you mean, taken?"

"When she and Sam were out, a van drove up and tried to get both of them inside. Sam only just escaped."

Jeremy stared into his mother's eyes, dumbstruck. He was at a loss for words. Taken? As in kidnapped? But why? His body frozen, his mind seemed to turn back on and burned with a hundred questions. His attention wandered back to Sam, and he was unclear what to do. Should he go over to him? Before he made up his mind, Devon walked through the door and sat on the bed. Jeremy couldn't hear her but assumed she was trying to provide reassurance.

"What's being done?" Jeremy asked. "Who's trying to find her?"

"We've already contacted the police," his mom said. "We filled out a report, and they said they'd call as soon as they had any information."

There was a knock on the door. Travis entered the room carrying a large brown bag. "I'm so sorry, Jess…. Where's Sam?"

Jeremy's mom pointed to the bedroom. Travis put the brown bag on the table and went into the room. Devon got up and came back to her mother's side; they stood arm in arm. The room was silent and still. No one seemed to know what to say.

Travis got up off the bed and wandered back to the main room. "Can we go to your room, Bob?"

Devon's dad nodded his head. "Sure."

"Kids. I need you to stay here," Travis said. "Take care of Sam." Jeremy and Devon both nodded. "There's some food in the bag." He indicated the bag he'd left on the table.

Once the adults left the room, Jeremy grabbed the food, and he and Devon went to join Sam. Devon sat on the bed next to him. Jeremy sat on the floor.

"I'm so sorry Sam," Jeremy said.

"Right," Sam said, his voice dripping with skepticism.

Warmth crept up Jeremy's chest and into his face. "Sam, I really am sorry. Not just for this, but for how I've been acting. I've been so worried that your mom would take mine away from me, but I didn't want to make my mom mad at me, so I've been taking it out on you, instead." Jeremy's words came out in a rush.

Silence followed. More for something to do with his hands than anything else, Jeremy began pulling baguette sandwiches and drinks out of the bag.

"Come on Sam, you need to eat," Devon said.

"I'm not hungry."

"Come have something to drink at least," she said.

Sam slid down off the bed onto the floor. Devon joined him. Jeremy handed Sam a bottle which he took but didn't open.

"What happened?" Devon asked.

Sam stared at his soda. He removed the cap from his soda then screwed it back on again.

"Mom and I were walking down the street. We'd just had lunch …" Tears welled up in Sam's eyes, but he took a steadying breath. "This van pulled up …"

Jeremy and Devon exchanged a look, but Sam had his head down, talking into the floor and didn't notice.

"... and grabbed mom…. She was closer to the street…. A man came at me, and I ran away…. I ran away from my mom…. I should have stayed…. I shouldn't have left her…." Sam broke into a sob. Devon reached over and put her arm around him. Sam didn't resist, though he sat stiffly at her side.

Jeremy was stunned. He couldn't imagine how awful it would be if it had been his own mom. His own mom ... This must be upsetting, no, terrible for her. Memories of how he'd been treating Sam and … Cheryl…. She didn't deserve to be snapped at when they were at the Louvre. She was just trying to help, but he had been so preoccupied with his own feelings, he hadn't worried about the effect of his behavior on the others.

Jeremy glanced at Sam whose face still shined with tears but who wasn't actively crying. Jeremy and Devon looked at each other, and she nodded slightly.

"Um, Sam," Jeremy said.

"Yeah?" Sam sat hunched, looking down at the floor.

"There's something Devon and I want to tell you…." Jeremy stopped, struggling to find the right words. "Here's the deal. And this is why we've been keeping to ourselves." Jeremy paused. "Okay, not completely. I know I've been a jerk to you cuz of our moms and it's not your fault. I just—"

Sam interrupted Jeremy's ramble. "What's the deal?" Although he cut Jeremy off, the iciness in Sam's voice had thawed. He wiped the tears from his face.

"We're in a secret club and there are some things we need to do but we can't—"

"Did that thing at your side just kick you?" Sam interrupted, his eyes wide and glued on Thing.

"I certainly did," Thing replied, causing Sam to lean away

from Jeremy.

"Thing!" Jeremy started.

But Thing continued. "Well, I heard you say you were going to tell him anyway, and you just used my name in a derogatory fashion."

"A derogatory … what?"

"Guys, stop," Devon said. "Sam, we're in a secret organization and these buddies we carry around with us are called magic buddies."

"No, we have actual names. I'm Birdbrain and that's—"

"Magic? … As in magic?" Sam glanced back and forth between Thing doing backflips and Birdbrain, who flapped her wings the moment he interrupted her.

"Yep." Birdbrain flapped her wings again. Thing bounced off Jeremy's leg.

"We're working on a case here in Paris," Devon continued. "And I'm wondering if it's not related to your mom's kidnapping."

"I'm not so sure about that," Jeremy said.

"What do you mean?" Devon asked.

Jeremy recounted how he saw his mom take something out of her backpack and give it to Travis at the airport after their bags went missing, and how his mom's backpack had been stolen at the park. "It almost seems like they're after my mom…. Cheryl is very important to her and maybe they took Cheryl to try to get something out of my mom…. But what?"

No one spoke for several minutes. Jeremy guessed that like him, Devon and Sam were deep in thought trying to figure out the why of it all.

"What does your mom do again?" Sam asked.

"Well, I thought she did computer research and design for Tech."

"What does that mean?" Sam asked.

"Not really sure, actually," Jeremy said. "And now I'm wondering if that's just a cover."

13. Disappeared

"What's the name of the company your parents work for?" Sam asked Jeremy and Devon as they continued to make their way through dinner.

"Technological Data ..." Jeremy's voice trailed away, as the truth hit him. Why hadn't he realized it before?

"...Consulting," Devon finished, staring wide-eyed at Jeremy. "How did we miss that?"

"I don't know … I mean, it's so obvious now," Jeremy said.

"What? What's obvious?" Sam tilted his head, his eyes narrowed.

"The initials for our parents' company are TDC ..." Jeremy said.

"... which also happen to be the initials for the organization we're in: The Travelers Detective Club," Devon said. "But what does that mean?" she added. "I mean, we knew there was some connection cuz Travis, Mr. Davis, is the head of their HR division. He told us last year he was second in command, I think that's what he called it, of the Travelers Detective Club."

"Maybe there's more to our parents' jobs than we thought," Jeremy said.

"Like you said, their jobs could be a cover for something." Sam said.

"Well," Jeremy replied, "Mom did say that their company monitors far-right extremist groups."

"What!" Devon choked on her soda.

"Oh, I forgot to tell you," Jeremy started and proceeded to fill her in on what he and Sam had overheard.

"But I don't really know what it means," Jeremy continued. "Does my mom just develop the technology to help monitor groups or does she spy on them? No," Jeremy said, incredulously, "she isn't the type ..." His voice trailed off.

"The type of what?" Devon asked.

"I don't know…. She just seems like an ordinary person." Maybe a bit too obsessed with being on time, though, he thought.

"In a world dominated by men she's done well in the world of tech … and she chose to become a single parent…. She seems incredibly smart and brave," Devon said.

"Or just plain crazy," Jeremy added. "Okay, what about your dad? Does he seem like he's keeping secrets from you and your mom?"

"Well, no. But then again, if he's good at his job we wouldn't notice, right? I had no idea Tech monitored hate groups. Could be my mom knows, and it's just me who doesn't," Devon said.

"What are you guys working on here in Paris," Sam asked.

Between them, Devon and Jeremy filled Sam in on everything they knew: the meaning behind the fairy tale, the stolen Monet, and the Sacré-Cœur's disappearance earlier that day. Jeremy also mentioned the van that tried to stop them and that a woman in the van was the same one who tried to deceive them in Portugal.

"Wait, so both people who tried to stop you in Portugal are now here in Paris?" Sam asked.

"Seems so," Jeremy said.

"How do we find my mom?" Sam asked.

At that moment the door from the hallway opened, and Jeremy's mom came in. "Devon, your mom and dad want you to go back to your hotel room."

"Okay." Devon balled up her trash and put it in the garbage. "I'll see you guys in the morning?"

"Yeah," Jeremy said.

After Devon left, Jeremy's mom joined Jeremy and Sam on the floor. She grabbed the last sandwich and soda from the bag.

"So what did Mr. Davis want?" Jeremy said.

"Does he have an idea of how to find my mom?" Sam said, his voice cracking.

"Mr. Davis wanted to talk about something work related." Jeremy's mom unwrapped her dinner. "The police are working on locating your mom, Sam." She put her hand on Sam's shoulder but quickly withdrew it.

She took a bite of her sandwich before continuing. "I need you guys to stay in tomorrow. With all that's happened to us, and …" she hesitated. "Mr. Davis said that something odd is happening in Paris."

"What do you mean something odd?" Jeremy asked.

His mom didn't answer right away. She appeared to be considering her words carefully. "Well, if you watch T.V. tomorrow you'll find out anyways. It seems that the Sacré-Cœur has disappeared."

Jeremy did his best to seem surprised. "Wait, what? How can something just disappear? That's impossible."

"Yeah, I'm not sure I believe it. But anyways, I need both of you to stay in tomorrow. It doesn't feel safe out—."

"Wait a second," Jeremy interrupted. "Mr. Davis says weird things are going on, a building supposedly disappears, and … what does that have to do with your work?"

"Why do you think it has anything to do with my work?"

"Because you said Mr. Davis wanted to talk to you about something work related, and then he told you about weird stuff happening in Paris."

Jeremy held his mom's gaze, and he could almost see her mind working. He threw caution to the wind.

"Does this have anything to do with the far-right extremist hate groups your company is tracking?"

Even if she didn't answer, the stunned look on her face was worth asking the question.

"So you guys heard our conversation?" She looked at Jeremy and Sam in turn.

They both nodded.

She sighed and took a moment to gather her thoughts. "We're not sure, but we're exploring that option."

Jeremy waited for more; this desire for information must have shown on his face.

"That's all I can say about it right now." She looked at her watch. "And it's late. We all need to try and get some sleep."

***

The next morning, after Jeremy's mom left for work, Devon came over. Sam was standing by the window looking outside when she came in. He gave her a weak smile and then returned his attention to the window.

"Did you guys sleep?" Devon asked.

Jeremy shook his head. "No."

Devon started to say something else, but Jeremy shook his head again. Devon nodded and seemed to understand. How they did or didn't sleep, and the crying Jeremy heard but respectfully ignored, wasn't something to talk about.

"What's your mom doing?" Jeremy asked.

"Interestingly enough, she went into work with dad."

"That is interesting," Jeremy said. "And I'm guessing she told you to stay here with us?"

"Yep. But really … stay inside a hotel room, when we could be roaming around Paris?" Devon said.

There was a knock on the door, and Jeremy opened it, welcoming Addie.

"You heard what happened?" Jeremy said.

"Yes, Travis told me. Hi Devon, Hi Sam…. Sorry about your mom…. Any news?"

Sam shook his head, his reddened eyes visible when he moved. Tears started running down his cheeks.

Jeremy walked over to Sam and embraced him in a hug. "Sam, I'm so, so sorry," Jeremy whispered in his ear. "We'll find her, I promise."

Jeremy let go of Sam and stepped awkwardly away.

"Thanks," Sam mumbled.

The room was silent for only a moment.

"Are you all ready to go?" Addie said.

"Go where?" Jeremy said. "Our parents were insistent that we stay here today."

"So?" Addie said.

"What do you mean, so?" Jeremy said.

"Are we members of the …" Addie broke off, glancing at Sam.

"It's okay," Jeremy said. "We told him."

"Great. So let's go," Addie said.

"Didn't you hear what I—" Jeremy started.

Devon interrupted. "I agree with Addie. We can't just sit here while Sam's mom is out there somewhere. Plus, Travis gave us a job to do, and we can't do it sitting here."

Jeremy tended to be a rule follower; being black in the US meant being overly scrutinized … any misstep could land him in trouble. Heck, he'd been assumed guilty even when he wasn't doing anything wrong. A few weeks back when he went off on his own at the store, an employee had asked if he planned to pay for an item in his hand. No one had ever approached his mom like that. And man, was his mom mad when she heard about it.

Despite this, it was hard to imagine staying inside all day when, like Devon said, Travis expected … but did he still expect or had that changed?

Sam turned away from the window and wiped his face with his hands. Taking a deep breath, he said, "I want to do whatever I can to help find my mom."

That did it for Jeremy. He wanted Sam to know he had his back. "Ok, I'm in."

"I figured we would go to the Eiffel Tower. That was next on the list, yes?" Addie opened the door and walked out of the hotel room.

"How's that going to help us find my mom?" Sam asked as he followed her out the door.

Everyone looked at Addie while the elevator approached. "I don't know," she said. She stepped into the elevator and turned to face the others. "But it feels better to do something than nothing, and that's all I can think of."

Everyone turned to Sam who shrugged in response.

"And maybe," Devon added, "if we find whoever stole the Sacré-Cœur, we'll find your mom."

Jeremy was the first out of the elevator. A man sat on a bench outside, peering over his newspaper at the entrance of the hotel. Jeremy recognized him as the man who locked eyes with him on the fifty-ninth floor before following Travis off of the observation deck the night of the company dinner. Jeremy quickly turned around and pushed everyone back into the elevator.

"Is there a garage exit?" Jeremy said, scanning the buttons.

Addie reached over and pushed the button marked SS, and the elevator opened next in an underground garage. They found the exit which brought them out on the side of the hotel. Jeremy peered around the corner. The man hadn't moved. Before Jeremy stepped back, the man turned his head.

"Oh crap, he saw me. We gotta go. Addie, which way?"

They took off running, following Addie who tore down side streets, parting crowds of people on sidewalks. Jeremy kept looking over his shoulder and after several minutes, he called out, "I think we've lost him."

Addie slowed down at his words. "There's a metro station up ahead."

Jeremy peeked over his shoulder one more time. "He's coming!" In the moment between Jeremy shouting out and turning around, he thought the man did something peculiar; he appeared to hit an imaginary wall. Jeremy did a double take. The man lay flat on his back. Questioning what he'd seen, and convincing himself the man must have tripped, Jeremy ran after the others.

They didn't stop until they were through the metro's turnstiles and down the escalator to the platform. Only when they were on the train with no sign of the man could Jeremy relax. The group spent the first few minutes catching their breath.

While Sam leaned over to talk to Addie, Jeremy's mind raced with questions. Who were these people and what did they want? What was his mom up to? Where was Cheryl, and how were they going to help find her?

Ten minutes later they exited the station and walked down the street. Around a corner the Eiffel Tower rose beside them.

"So this secret organization you're all in," Sam said, "what do you actually do?"

"Try and fix stuff like this," Jeremy said.

"Yeah, but how?"

"Not sure. I'll let you know when we figure it out." Jeremy smiled at Sam to let him know he wasn't intentionally holding back information.

"Wow," Jeremy continued. "There sure is a lot of security around." Soldiers in fatigues, carrying military style assault rifles, were patrolling in groups of twos and threes.

"What did you expect," Addie said, "after everything that has happened."

"Yeah, I guess. It's just different seeing it up close." In truth, the sight unsettled Jeremy.

A sign stated that the stairs and elevators were closed indefinitely. Because of this, tourists were milling about, staring up at the tower, seemingly lost as to what to do.

"It's so beautiful," Devon said.

Despite the tension in the air, the weather was almost perfect. Puffy clouds dotted the sky but didn't block the sun.

"I can't imagine them getting past all this security and …" Devon's voice trailed off. For the Eiffel Tower had vanished. Screams penetrated the air around them, and the scene descended into pandemonium.

14. Captured

"Look around for those two guys!" Devon yelled. All four of them spun around, scanning the surrounding area.

"Is that them?" Sam pointed at two figures heading down the stairs toward a flotilla of tourist boats. The two men jumped onto a boat pulling away from the dock.

"Yes, it is!" shouted Jeremy.

"We'll never get them," Devon said exasperatedly. "Plus, they might have a gun. What?"

Birdbrain was pecking at her leg and flapping her wings. "Throw me."

"What?"

"Throw me," Birdbrain repeated. "I think I have a new power in me just like Napoleon."

"Throw you where?" Devon asked.

"Toward that boat."

"Are you crazy?" Devon said.

"Just do it," Thing called out from Jeremy's side.

Devon unclipped Birdbrain, leaving the carabiner clip on her pants.

"Just throw me up in the air. If I'm wrong, just come and get me."

"What are you going to do?" Devon asked.

"No idea. I'll just wing it."

"Ha ha. Good one," Thing said.

"Go for the hat," Addie chimed in.

"Hurry," Jeremy called out. "They're getting away."

Devon drew her arm back and launched Birdbrain into the air. Birdbrain flapped her wings but sank down toward the ground. Devon started to run after her, but Birdbrain gained altitude and flew after the boat.

Devon started running along the path after her, weaving in and out of panicked tourists. Jeremy, Addie and Sam did their best to follow close behind. After pushing through a thick wall of people, they emerged just in time to see Birdbrain swipe the hat off of the shorter man and turn back their way. The taller man, slow to react, swatted at Birdbrain but missed.

"That was so much fun!" Birdbrain exclaimed after dropping the hat in Devon's hand and landing on her shoulder. "The man has the miniature Eiffel Tower in his hand. Let me go back."

"Ok." Sam plucked Birdbrain off Devon.

"No!" Devon said anxiously.

But it was too late. Sam had already launched Birdbrain into the air, and she flew away, flapping her wings with enthusiasm.

Devon turned on Sam. "Why did you do that? She's not yours! And how can she get the tower if it's in his hand? She'll get caught."

"Devon, relax," Jeremy said, siding with Sam. "He just wanted to help. She'll be fine."

"No, she won't," Addie said.

The taller man had Birdbrain in his hand.

"Oh no, oh no, oh no," Devon cried, tears forming in her eyes.

Devon, Jeremy, Sam and Addie watched the boat drift down the Seine, taking Birdbrain with it. Around them, some people were running past while others stood still, apparently dazed by the disappearance of the Eiffel Tower.

"We have to go to phase two," Addie said.

"What's phase two?" Sam asked.

"Yeah, we didn't talk about a phase two," Jeremy said.

"That's because I just made it up," Addie said. "While they're on the boat, let's get to their hotel and find the other things they stole."

"Other things, things, things," Thing said. "Why, oh why did I have to get such a name?"

"Because you were being a pain at the time, in case you don't remember," Jeremy said. "Now, come on."

"What do you mean come on? I'm attached to you, you dimwitted, insufferable nincompoop."

"Guys, come on!" Devon called over her shoulder. She and Addie were already thirty feet ahead.

Jeremy and Sam caught up to Devon and Addie who led them to the metro. They jumped onto a train, slipping sideways through the closing doors. No one dared talk, but the four kept exchanging glances. Once on the street, they ran flat out.

"Let me … go in." Addie said. "I … am French and … will fit in and—"

"We're … not … arguing." Devon clutched at her side. "Plus, you … have the … key. Go."

Once in front of the hotel, Addie paused before entering with her shoulders squared and head held high, exuding confidence.

"She's got guts," Sam said.

"Yeah, she does," Jeremy said.

"That's gross," Thing said.

"It's not what you … oh never mind," Jeremy said.

"That thing is pretty funny," Sam remarked.

"I am not *a* thing, my name is Thing. Please don't confuse the two."

Sam laughed. Jeremy realized Devon wasn't next to him anymore. She was sitting off to the side, on the edge of a plantar box, gazing down at the ground. Jeremy went and sat down next to her.

"Hey, I'm sorry about Birdbrain. We'll get her back."

"We will," Thing added.

"Thanks, guys," Devon said, wiping her eyes. "Hey, Sam, come here. I know you were only trying to help, and knowing Birdbrain she would have found a way to take off on her own."

"I am sorry Devon," Sam said.

"I know," she replied. "It's … oh. Addie's back."

"Get over here," Jeremy said, grabbing Devon and pulling her further off to the side. "Sam," he whispered urgently. "Come here!"

"What—?" Sam swallowed his words when Jeremy pointed to a man striding toward the hotel. The man glanced at Addie walking past, and did a double take. He must have recognized his backpack because he started after her.

"Hey," the man said. "Hey, you. Come back here."

"Run, Addie!" Sam yelled.

All four of them took off running, Jeremy waiting until Addie had caught up, but the man wasn't far behind.

"Stop for a second," Thing said to Jeremy.

"What? Are you crazy, I'm not—"

But Thing persisted. "Let me show you my new power."

Despite his urge to run, Jeremy couldn't help himself. He turned to face the man, thirty feet away, when suddenly the man appeared to run into an invisible wall. He fell back onto the pavement, stunned.

"Okay, now you can run," Thing said.

Jeremy gaped at Thing. "Did you—?"

"Run!" Thing repeated. Jeremy turned to take off after his friends, but the man he had seen in front of the hotel that morning stepped out from behind a building.

"Devon!" Jeremy yelled. But at that moment someone grabbed him from behind, pinning his arms to his chest while the man in front grabbed Jeremy's legs. They carried him to a van parked with its motor running. Jeremy thought he heard Sam shouting but couldn't be sure. Thrown into the back of the van, the door slid shut, and he was plunged into darkness.

Jeremy jumped to his feet, banging his head on the roof of the van. He dropped back down to the floor and scurried to the side of the van, holding his head, adrenaline giving way to fear. He needed something to lean against to feel more grounded. His eyes adjusted to the darkness. There was a metal partition between the back section of the van and the driver's area. He was caged in. Jeremy started to panic. What was he going to do? It felt like they were driving around forever, but it might have only been a few minutes. He felt so alone and scared.... Alone.

"Thing? Are you still here."

"Yeah, I'm here. But what's going on?"

"I'm not sure. But I'm really scared."

"I can tell, your voice is shaking … it's like you're—"

"Thing, I can't handle jokes now."

"But—"

"We're stopping. What should I do?"

Before Thing could respond, the side door of the van opened. Jeremy covered his eyes from the glare of the sun; they protested the sudden and extreme contrast of light. Someone reached in and roughly grabbed the arm that wasn't blocking his eyes.

"Come on," a voice demanded.

Jeremy remained silent while he was marched into a building, his legs feeling like jelly. His eyes darted from left to right but saw nothing familiar. Into an elevator, up to the third floor. Out the elevator and down the hall. The man holding him pulled out a key card and opened a door. He pushed Jeremy into the room and closed it behind him, not entering himself. Jeremy turned around to face the door. It slammed in his face.

"Jeremy?" a voice behind him called.

He whipped around. "Cheryl?"

Cheryl strode up to him and enveloped him in a hug which he returned.

"What's happening? How?... Why?... How did they get you?" Cheryl stammered.

"I was out with the others," Jeremy said, not wanting to get into specifics. "We must have been followed.... How are you? Are you okay?"

Before she could answer, the door to the room opened, and a woman strode in.

"You!" Jeremy exclaimed.

15. The Woman From Portugal

"Yes, me." The woman whom Jeremy had met in Portugal, the one he and Devon had tricked in the end, stood in front of him.

"Wait," Cheryl said, staring at Jeremy before her eyes darted to the woman and then back again. "You know her?"

"We've met." The sentence hung in the air, waiting for an addendum, some type of explanation that Jeremy did not want to give.

"But we have not been properly introduced," the woman said with a smirk. "My name is Heinke—"

"What do you want?" Jeremy interrupted.

Her smirk grew larger as if she was amused. "Your mother has something that I need."

"My mom?...You must be mistaken."

"No, I'm not. She has an SD card with the second half of an encrypted code that will allow me to ..." Heinke stopped herself. "What it does is not important. What is important is that she delivers it if she wants to see either of you again."

Her eyes raked over Jeremy and Cheryl with disdain. "Though perhaps she could do better ..." Heinke turned up her nose as if they smelled.

Her contemptuous words and attitude landed like a sucker punch to Jeremy's gut. Anger and incredulity rose from his pain. "What's that supposed to mean?"

"Families are supposed to match." Heinke's eyes were ablaze but she spoke with a calm conviction more appropriate for one reviewing what to have for dinner. "Blacks and whites shouldn't be together and as for her..." she looked at Cheryl up and down, "...none of this is natural."

"Are you kidding me!" Jeremy yelled, taking a step forward.

Cheryl placed her hand gently on Jeremy's shoulder. "Leave it, Jeremy."

Heinke smiled maliciously and turned toward the door.

"Oh, you're one of them." Jeremy couldn't help himself. He knew he should probably keep his mouth shut, but this type of talk always riled him. "So in other words, you want white, straight people to rule the world. Right."

Cheryl groaned.

Heinke didn't respond and closed the door behind her.

"How do you know her?" Cheryl asked.

Jeremy did not answer immediately. His mind raced, bouncing between ideas of what was so important about an SD card, why and how his mother was involved, where he and Cheryl were, and how they were going to get out of their predicament. What could he say to Cheryl about this woman? He couldn't reveal information about the TDC.

"Jeremy?"

Jeremy's eyes darted back and forth across the room, not because he wanted to find a way out, though he did, but because his mind searched for something to say. "We ran into her in Portugal last summer…." Jeremy paused to give himself time. The idea came slowly to him. "She … she harassed mom and I for being together. She didn't like that our skin colors didn't match. I thought she was just some random woman …

but perhaps she was following Mom." Jeremy looked at Cheryl for the first time, and it seemed that she bought his story.

"What is your mom involved in?"

"I don't know.... Well, she told you the other morning about following extremist hate groups." In response to Cheryl's raised eyebrows he added, "Yeah, we listened at the door."

"Of course you did. Jeremy, where is Sam?"

"I'm not sure." Seeing the concern on Cheryl's face, Jeremy added, "But he's okay. He's with the others, and they weren't taken, only me."

Jeremy and Cheryl stared at one another for several moments. Jeremy started looking around the room.

"Do you have any idea where we are?" He walked to the small window and peered outside. He could see down to the street, but only nondescript buildings surrounded them.

Cheryl shook her head slightly. "No. I think this is a converted storage room. And I'm guessing we're in some kind of office building."

"What about .... How many people are watching this room?"

"When I've had to go to the bathroom there's been just one man who takes me."

"Where's the bathroom?"

"At the end of the hall."

"Is it near the elevator?"

"No ... but I saw an exit sign ... for the stairs perhaps. Why?"

"Just thinking," Jeremy said.

"Jeremy, the only thinking you need to do is where you want to go in Paris once we get out of here."

"And who's going to rescue us? No one knows we're here."

"I'm sure the police are working to track us down."

"The police?" Jeremy shook his head. "Sorry, but I've learned not to trust them."

"We're not in the states and they're not—"

Jeremy cut her off. "I don't want to have that conversation with you." His tone was dismissive, and he wondered if he'd been too abrupt.

They stared at each other, Jeremy determined not to break eye contact first. Cheryl held his gaze, her expression softening.

"Jeremy. This isn't the states, and who else is there?" She paused, walking up to and staring out of the window. After a moment, she turned to face him. "We don't know if they're armed or what they're capable of."

An idea formed in Jeremy's mind, but what he couldn't figure out was how to convince Cheryl to trust him without giving anything away. "We need a diversion."

"Jeremy, this isn't some kids' game."

"I know." Again he met her gaze and held it.

"And then what?" Cheryl asked.

"We run."

Cheryl sighed. "Jeremy. I appreciate that you want to find a way to get us out of this, but running isn't really a plan. We need to wait for—"

"Surely Mom told you I'm not the patient type."

Cheryl cracked a smile. "So I've heard…. But Jeremy, this is serious."

"I know."

They sat on the floor, leaning against a wall. Jeremy got up to look out the window every ten minutes or so, hoping something would look familiar or some plan would come to him.

"Sam's alright you know," Jeremy said, breaking the silence.

"What?"

"I said, 'Sam's alright.'"

Cheryl smiled. "Are you guys getting along better?"

"Yeah. I've just been so jealous of you … and I knew I couldn't say anything, so I took it out on Sam."

"Jeremy, it's okay to say that you're jealous. It's completely normal."

Jeremy met Cheryl's gaze, as an awkward silence descended, before peering at the ground. A moment later, he got up yet again to stare out the window.

"Hey."

"What?" Cheryl got up to join him.

"Heinke and one of the men who took me just got into that van." Jeremy turned to Cheryl. "That means there's only one man left to watch us."

Cheryl and Jeremy stared at each other.

"Jeremy don't," Cheryl said.

"When you hear a diversion," Jeremy backed away from Cheryl," run for the stairs."

"Jeremy, no!" She reached for his arm.

Jeremy dodged Cheryl's grasp and opened the door. A man leaned against the wall, looking at his phone, two doors down. He looked up when Jeremy stepped out.

"Bathroom," Jeremy said.

"This way." The man indicated that Jeremy should go toward him.

Jeremy saw that there were exit signs on both ends of the corridor.

"You ready, Thing?" Jeremy whispered.

"I was born ready."

Jeremy looked down at Thing, remembering how Thing had jumped all around his room when they first met. "Yeah, you were."

"Thanks," Jeremy called out to the man down the hall, "but I'll go this way."

He took off running in the opposite direction.

"Jeremy, no!" Cheryl cried out from the doorway.

Jeremy sprinted down the corridor. After fifteen steps he glanced over his shoulder. The man sprinted after them and was closing in.

"Now!" Jeremy told Thing.

A second later the man bounced against an invisible wall, his expression one of shock before he fell back to the floor, hitting his head and momentarily stunned. Jeremy turned around and ran back toward Cheryl. "Come on!"

Together they ran to the end of the hall and down the stairs. Three floors down, Jeremy opened the door but stepped back quickly, pulling the door closed.

"They're back already," he whispered to Cheryl. Had the man upstairs come to and called them back? Or had the woman just gotten something out of the van, and it hadn't actually gone anywhere? He opened the door a crack. The woman had a large brown bag in her hand and approached the elevator. The van drove away. It took a moment for the elevator to come, and when it did, the woman got in.

Jeremy stepped out from behind the door only to have the woman step back out of the elevator—the door hadn't closed—and with her stood the man from upstairs.

Jeremy froze.

The man inched aside his coat to reveal a holstered gun. Jeremy gulped and knew he was out of options. He and Cheryl went back into the elevator.

"You're just in time for lunch," Heinke smirked, holding up the bag.

16. Teamwork

"What's so important about an SD card, and why do you think my mom has it?" Jeremy's curiosity wouldn't let him keep quiet. "You said it had half of an encrypted code … for what? What could be so important you'd kidnap and threaten us?"

Heinke absentmindedly fingered a locket around her neck. Dropping her hand, she spoke, as if reciting a speech. "The world is being taken over by miscreants and intruders who don't belong. The rightful leaders are being pushed out. Lawlessness and disorder have become the norm. We must usher in new leadership that will restore the world order."

147

"And my mom has something that will help you achieve this new world order? Put two codes together and what? You suddenly have some great superpower ... or a map to something that will give you that power?" The woman's eyes grew wide, but she didn't respond. "That's it, isn't it? These codes, when put together, will lead you to something ..." Jeremy's voice trailed off. They had made it back to the room. Jeremy and Cheryl were ushered inside.

Heinke handed them the brown bag. "Someone has to do something, and with this completed code, I will have the power to rule the world." She closed the door.

"That lady's a nutcase," Jeremy said. He resumed his place on the floor, leaning against the wall.

Cheryl joined him, pulling out and unwrapping baguette sandwiches. "Yes, she is. But Jeremy, you need to be careful. We don't know what these people are capable of."

"I know. But we can't just sit here and wait. This lady is crazy. And what if whatever she gets from my mom gives her power? What then? We have to stop her."

"Jeremy, like you said, she's crazy. There's no such thing. She's talking about bringing codes together, and ... she's talking about magic like it's real."

Jeremy bit into his sandwich, unclear about what to say or do next. He looked down at his side and eyed Thing who had kicked him. It took a moment for him to realize that Thing was red; another magic buddy was nearby. Jeremy jumped up, dropping his partially eaten turkey and cheese sandwich on the floor, and went to the window. He searched the street.

"I have to go to the bathroom," he said.

Cheryl eyed him questioningly.

"Seriously. I'll be back, promise."

Jeremy opened the door and peeked out. The man sat in a chair just outside the door.

"I have to go to the bathroom … really."

The man led Jeremy down the hall, holding onto his arm and making sure Jeremy walked through the bathroom door. Once inside a stall, Jeremy addressed Thing. "You're red."

"Yep."

"That means Napoleon is here."

"Yep."

"Which means we need to create a diversion."

"Yep."

"Can you please say something more than yep?"

"Okay." Thing stared at Jeremy mischievously but said nothing else.

"Is there ever a time serious enough that you can't make a joke?"

"Nope." Thing's eyes sparkled.

"You can't be up on this floor," the man said from the hallway.

A familiar voice said, "Sorry."

Jeremy stepped out of the stall, swung open the bathroom door and came face to face with Devon. They stared at each other; Jeremy shook his head, trying to do so imperceptibly. Jeremy wanted to get back to Cheryl before the man realized these were his friends.

But Sam said, "Jeremy!"

"Wait, you know—?"

Jeremy took off running, hoping the man would chase him again. Instead he heard a scream.

"I'd stop if I were you."

Jeremy skidded to a halt and turned around. The man had drawn his gun and pointed it at Jeremy. Jeremy froze, fear immobilizing him. They stared at each other for a moment.

"Come back here, now," the man demanded.

"Okay, okay. But can you please put that away. It's freaking me out."

"You're in no position to make demands."

The door between Jeremy and the man opened, and Cheryl stuck her head out. She looked at Jeremy, then the man with the gun and then Sam, Addie and Devon behind him.

"Sam!" Cheryl stammered. "What?"

They all froze for a moment. Worry flitted in the man's eyes, possibly because they outnumbered him, though he had a gun. With difficulty, Jeremy made himself walk back toward the man.

"Everyone inside," the man demanded, stepping back so they were all in front of him.

Sam reached the door first, giving his mom a hug. Devon and Jeremy reached the door together. Jeremy let Devon go first and saw the man holster his gun after Addie moved toward the door. Out of the corner of his eye, Jeremy saw movement once the man's hand was off his gun. A chair flew through the air and hit the man in the head with such speed it knocked him over.

"Merci, Napoleon!" Addie said.

"Everyone, let's go!" Jeremy shouted.

He reached down and hesitated a moment before grabbing the man's gun. Jeremy didn't realize how much guns scared him until he was about to touch one. And it was heavier than he'd imagined.

"Jeremy, what are you doing?" Devon cried.

Without answering, he walked quickly with it to the bathroom, where he dropped it in the toilet.

He burst out of the bathroom and almost hit Sam. They all ran toward the exit with Jeremy last through the door. He turned back before the door closed. The man lay immobile on the floor. Five sets of feet thundered down the stairs. Cheryl, having waited for Jeremy, scolded him for picking up the gun. "And it's not like he can't just get it out of the toilet," she finished.

They burst out onto the ground floor lobby. "Yeah," Jeremy said, "but I hadn't flushed the toilet."

Outside on the sidewalk, Devon looked right and left. "Where to now?" she asked.

"We need to call the police." Cheryl peered down the street perhaps hoping to see an officer driving by.

Before anyone could answer, a woman's voice said, "You are proving to be more trouble than you're worth."

Jeremy turned toward the voice. Heinke and the second man approached them.

"What are you going to do, kill us all?" Jeremy was done with this woman and her attitude.

"Jeremy!" Both Cheryl and Devon attempted to shush him.

"What! There are five of us and two of them."

"And they are armed," Cheryl said. "Jeremy, please."

"Yes, listen to her, Jeremy," Heinke sneered, "and come back inside."

Addie sidled up to Jeremy and whispered, "Stall her."

"We're not going back inside," Jeremy said.

"Oh, yes you are." Heinke's voice dripped with malice and spite. Her eyes were rageful, fiery.

"Deitrich," she said to the man next to her.

Deitrich pulled out a gun and pointed it at the group. Fear rippled through them in a wave. Frozen, no one moved for several moments.

Three police cars came skidding to a halt in front of them, and six police officers jumped out, guns drawn. They did not have to say anything for Deitrich to put his gun down on the ground and his hands in the air. Heinke stood, silent and fuming.

Addie smiled at Cheryl. "I did call the police."

"Excuse me, officer. Excuse me," Jeremy called out to the police officers taking the miscreants to the patrol car.

The officer leading Heinke away turned around.

"That woman stole my mother's locket. She's wearing it around her neck."

"What? That's not true! It's mine!" Heinke shrieked.

The officer looked from Heinke to Jeremy and back again.

"If you open it, there's an SD card inside," Jeremy said.

Heinke's eyes grew wide. The officer took the necklace off of her and opened the locket, nodded and closed it again. He stepped forward and handed it to Jeremy.

Jeremy took the locket, and putting it in his pocket, smiled at Heinke, whose face contorted in rage.

"You!" Heinke spat at Jeremy. "You'll be … I'm going … It's not …" she stammered as the policeman grabbed her arm.

Jeremy turned away from her. "Addie, can you get us out of here?"

17. The SD Card

Heading back to the metro, Devon, Jeremy, and Addie walked behind Sam and Cheryl who were strolling arm in arm.

"How did you find us?" Jeremy asked quietly, not wanting Cheryl to hear.

"We followed you," Devon said.

"I figured that. But how?"

"It was Addie's idea. Well," Devon paused, "and Napoleon's too. Remember, the hotel was close to the Sacré-Cœur. When you called out, Addie realized you were being kidnapped, and … Addie, you tell him what happened."

"Napoleon did it, really. I froze at first, but then Napoleon whinnied, and that brown horse came running around the corner. It hadn't gone back to the carousel."

"Where is it now?" Jeremy looked up into the sky.

"I told it to go back," Napoleon said sadly.

"You should have seen Sam," Devon chuckled. "When the horse came around the corner, his jaw dropped nearly to the ground, but he recovered pretty quickly."

Jeremy smiled at the image. Walking past a bakery whose sweet smells wafted onto the sidewalk, Jeremy's stomach grumbled. He hadn't finished his sandwich. While contemplating whether or not to stop for food, he noticed the bag on Addie's back.

"Is that the backpack from the man's hotel room?" he asked. "Does it have everything in it?"

"I haven't even looked yet. We were so focused on following you," Addie said.

"Let's not open it now, when Cheryl's here," Devon said.

"I wonder if your parents will be okay with you touring Paris," Addie said.

"Well, they don't know about the other man," Jeremy said. "And the people who took Cheryl and me have been apprehended, so I don't see why we can't convince them it's safe."

"Then let's meet tomorrow."

When Jeremy walked into the hotel room, followed by Cheryl and Sam, his mom ran to him.

"Jeremy! Oh, thank goodness you're okay."

She enveloped him in a gigantic hug, squeezing him so hard and long that he eventually said, "Mom … Mom … You're squishing me.…"

His mom released him and stared hard into his eyes. "You're okay?"

He nodded.

"When Mr. Davis called and told me you'd been taken ..." Her voice cracked and she took a deep breath. "You promise you're okay?"

"Yeah, promise." He gave her a smile hoping to reassure her. She held onto his shoulders, searching his eyes with hers before wrapping him in a hug again.

"Mom."

"Yeah?"

"I'm okay, really. And it's okay. You can let go of me, and say hi to Cheryl. I know you were scared for her too."

His mom squeezed him tight before pulling away, meeting

his gaze. Jeremy smiled. She kissed him on the cheek and then turned to embrace Cheryl.

Later that night, after dinner, Jeremy cornered his mom while Cheryl and Sam were spending time together.

"Mom, what is it that you do for Tech? I mean, really?"

His mom didn't say anything at first, and Jeremy could almost hear her thinking. "I'm sorry, Jeremy. But I can't tell you more than you already know."

"I saw you give Mr. Davis something out of your backpack at the airport. It was the SD card that woman, Heinke, wanted, wasn't it?"

"Yes, it was."

"And she said crazy things like if she combined codes from two SD cards they would reveal a map where she could find something that would help her rule the world."

His mom stood silent, watching him.

What isn't Mom telling me? Jeremy thought. "What would tech do if they had that map?" he said out loud. "Would they try to take over? Is that what you're trying to do?" His tone was at first curious, but changed to worry and ended up sounding accusatory by his last question.

"Jeremy, I'm not sure what would happen if the two

encrypted codes came together. But what she's talking about is crazy talk. It's as if she thinks she'd find something magical. Most likely it would reveal some state secret that would be helpful in overthrowing a government. But no. Tech would not use that information. We try to stop people who would do that."

Jeremy cut in. "But if Tech had the map would they destroy whatever they found?"

"Yes," his mom nodded. "That is what we would try and do. But first we have to find Heinke's card, and she won't give up its location easily."

Jeremy stared at his mom.

"What?" she asked. "You look as if you don't believe me."

"I … Why didn't you ever tell me what you really did for work? That you were tracking extremist hate groups?"

His mom was quiet for a moment. Taking a deep breath she said, "You have to understand, Jeremy. When I started working for Tech, you were much younger. I didn't want to scare you with talk of extremist hate groups, and so I told you our cover story. And then it became easier to keep to that same story, and there was never a time when I felt I needed to tell you what I really did." She sounded worried he wouldn't understand.

They held each other's gaze. Jeremy recognized his mother's love and concern.

Jeremy reached into his pocket and pulled out the locket the police officer took from Heinke. He held his hand out, palm up, with the locket in his hand.

"What's that?"

"Open it."

She eyed him quizzically before opening the locket. Inside lay an SD card. The look of incredulity on his mom's face made Jeremy grin.

"How did you …?"

"She went into this crazy speech, and at one point when I asked about the SD card, she fingered her locket. So when the police took her away, I claimed that she had stolen the locket from you. I guessed it had an SD card inside, and after the officer checked, he gave it to me."

"Wow … Jeremy…. This is huge." She enveloped him in yet another hug. "I've said it before, but I'll say it again." She pulled him away so she could look him in the eyes. "You are one amazing kid."

"Thanks, Mom."

***

They got a late start the next day. Jeremy's mom took the morning off from work. She and Jeremy, along with Sam and Cheryl, cuddled on the queen bed and watched a movie, the moms holding tight to their sons.

When Jeremy and Sam finally extricated themselves, they picked up Devon next door and headed off to meet Addie. Devon called earlier to warn her of their delay.

"We need to get back to the site of the Sacré-Cœur," Addie said by way of a welcome.

"Why?" Sam asked.

"We can use the horse to help us return all of this quickly."

"But what about the Eiffel Tower and Birdbrain?" Devon said anxiously.

"I'm not sure yet. Let's do one thing at a time, yes?" Addie said. Once seated on the train, Addie pulled a piece of paper from the backpack and held it up to the group. "This explains it."

"What explains what?" Jeremy asked.

"I could not figure out why the taller man did not just take the hat. Did he and the other man make an agreement? But this looks to be a translation of the fairy tale I read to you before.

And it is incorrect."

"How's that?" Sam asked.

"This one says that only the man with the hat can harness the powers. That if someone takes the hat from him, it will break apart. There is nothing about the townspeople using the hat to return him to the pillar."

"How do we know which version is right?"

"Where's the hat, Devon?" Addie asked.

Devon pulled the hat out of her pocket. "Here." She pulled out a brown cap, rounded on the top with a visor. "And that means that the version you read is the correct one."

"But I suspect that now he knows, the man will want it back," Addie said.

"Can I see inside the bag?" Jeremy asked.

Addie opened the backpack and held it out. Jeremy spotted miniature figurines, about four or five inches tall, of the Sacré-Cœur, the art stolen from the Louvre and the Musée d'Orsay. There was also a tree.

"I thought a tree disappeared the other day," he remarked when he had finished examining the contents of the bag.

"So there's a problem," Sam said. The other three turned to him, and he continued. "We can't go up on a flying horse in the middle of the day, can we?"

Jeremy turned to Devon. "Ready for another nighttime flight?"

"Too bad Birdbrain isn't here," Devon remarked. "She's been ready for a year." She turned to Addie. "What should we do while we wait? It's too early to go to the carousel." She looked at her watch. "It's only two o'clock."

"Well, there's a lot to see in the general area of Montmartre. We could easily spend the day there."

"As long as there's food involved," Sam said.

"Yep, that," seconded Jeremy.

18. A Nighttime Flight

The group exited the metro station and meandered up the street, coming upon a scene vastly different from that of the day before. There were no artists painting and selling their work. Handfuls of tourists wandered around but appeared lost; there was no longer a grand Catholic basilica to tour.

Two long flights of stairs above them, at the site of the missing Sacré-Cœur, police patrolled the area, keeping curiosity seekers away.

"We need to have a plan," Addie said once they reached the carousel.

"We need to place the Sacré-Cœur back in the middle of the area, put the hat on, and wish for it to be its original size." Devon turned to Addie. "That's all we have to do, right?"

"I think so. I hope so."

"How are we going to get past the police?" Jeremy asked. "We can't just walk up there."

"We are using the horse, remember." Napoleon said.

"Yeah, but don't ya think the police will notice when we fly overhead?

"As Birdbrain would say, let's just wing it," Thing said.

They turned away and meandered down cobblestone streets looking in store windows, wandering through a cemetery, perusing t-shirt and souvenir shops. Jeremy had hoped it would keep his mind occupied, but he couldn't help worrying about what they were going to try and do that night. So much had gone wrong on this trip, and he couldn't help feeling that their bad luck hadn't run out.

"Hey," Jeremy said, "did either of your parents mention that we should be back for dinner?"

Sam and Devon shook their heads.

"Let's call the hotel and leave a message saying we're going to dinner with Addie," Devon said. "At least so they don't worry."

Addie pulled out her cell phone. "Here, use this."

"Your parents let you have a cell phone?" Jeremy said. "Dang. My mom says I have to wait until I'm older."

"How old?" Sam asked.

"I've never been able to pin her down exactly. I need to work on that."

"Well, it's useful. It's why the police came so soon yesterday," Addie said.

While Devon called the hotel, Jeremy stood to the side watching Sam out of the corner of his eye. He wasn't so bad really—pretty fun to be around, actually. Jeremy decided it was time to give Sam a break.

"Hey, Sam," Jeremy said, walking up to him.

"Yeah?"

"What do you think about ganging up on our moms, convincing them to get us both cell phones?"

Sam smiled, but before he could answer, Devon was off the phone.

"Okay," Devon said. "I talked to my dad, and he checked in with your moms too. They weren't too keen on the idea at first after what happened yesterday. But Travis has them working late, and I promised we'd all stay together and get back to the hotel by nine o'clock.

"Will that give us enough time?" Addie asked.

Jeremy shrugged. "Let's not worry about that now."

"The sun is going down," Devon said. "Once it's dark we'll grab the horse, and no one will see us."

They had made it back to the large open courtyard below the Sacré-Cœur.

"Um guys." Jeremy was staring at the carousel. "Where's the horse?"

"What?" Addie said.

"The horse is missing." Jeremy motioned to a gap in the carousel.

"Oh no," Addie said.

"What's that up on the hill?" Sam pointed to a forested area behind the carousel. Jeremy squinted and could see the outline of a horse grazing under the trees.

"Wait," Sam said, turning his gaze from the horse to the carousel and back again. "This is … from there? I thought you guys were kidding yesterday. I thought ... actually, I don't know what I thought."

"Yes. It is, what do you Americans say? Awesome." Napoleon flicked his tail.

The group walked up to the horse and sat down. They waited in the cover of the trees for it to get dark. Thirty minutes later they decided it was time. Unfortunately, street lights surrounding the site of the Sacré-Cœur flickered on, and their plan to use the cover of darkness was stymied.

"We just have to go for it," Jeremy said. "If we don't do it now, when can we?"

Quietly, one by one, they nodded in agreement.

Devon returned the backpack to Addie after taking out the miniature Sacré-Cœur. As she put on the hat, Jeremy caught her arm. "Don't get too attached to that. I don't want you turned to stone."

"I won't." Devon hopped up on the horse. "Come on." Jeremy, Addie and Sam followed her.

"Your turn," Addie said to Napoleon, and after he whinnied, they launched into the air. They rose up out of the trees until they could see the empty area where the basilica once stood.

"I count six policemen." Sam said. "They're in groups of two."

"How do we keep them away from the Sacré-Cœur once I put it down?" Devon asked.

"Why does it matter, once we're out of there?" Sam asked.

"Because if they're too close, they'll be killed," Devon said.

Jeremy felt Thing kick him in the side. "What?" Jeremy said.

"Remember what I did earlier?"

"Oh, right." Jeremy spoke louder. "Guys, Thing has a new magic power that can help us."

Addie looked back at Jeremy and Devon, who nodded their heads, and Addie gave Napoleon the command. They flew over and down to the site. Devon jumped off the horse and placed the miniature structure on the ground, causing a chorus of shouts to permeate the air. She jumped back on the horse, but the police were closing in.

"Come on, Thing," Jeremy shouted.

"I'm too far away. Napoleon," Thing said, "I need the horse to fly closer to those guys."

"Closer?" Sam said incredulously. "Are you crazy?"

But Napoleon had already let out a whinny, and the horse they were riding headed straight for the closest two policemen running toward them. Suddenly the two men hit an invisible wall and were thrown back fifteen feet. While the policemen lay dazed on the ground, the group flew in a circular pattern to the next pair and did the same. Flying toward the third pair, Jeremy realized they were too close to the miniature Sacré-Cœur. But before he could say anything, they too had fallen over.

"We have to move them out of the way," Jeremy said. "They're too close."

The horse descended next to the men, and everyone jumped off and dragged the policemen farther away. But at the same time, the others started to stir.

"Oh no." Addie pointed at the officers sitting up. "This will never work."

"Yes, it will." Devon jumped up on the horse. "Come on everyone."

They all vaulted onto the horse, and as it ascended, Jeremy peered over his shoulder. Devon's eyes were intense and focused downward. He twisted back around. The model of the basilica was getting bigger, but it took thirty seconds for the

Sacré-Cœur to regain its full size. Devon magically enlarged the church but gave the officers a chance to get out of the way.

"Now we just have to return the artworks," Addie said, as they flew away from the scene.

"And there's a tree," said Jeremy.

"Where's that from?" Devon asked.

"From near the Eiffel Tower. I saw it disappear when Sam and I were there, but I thought I was seeing things."

"Why do you always have to say that!" Thing complained.

"Thing, not now," Jeremy said.

"Why did you call him Thing?" Napoleon asked. "Wait. Is that your name? No wonder you did not want to tell me before."

"Shut it, Horsey," Thing replied.

"My name is not Horsey, it is—"

"Can we focus please," Devon commanded. "Where should we put the artwork?"

"It would be easier if we just put it all in one place," Jeremy said.

"How about outside a police station?" Sam asked.

"I'd really rather not get caught being out late at a police station, if you don't mind," Jeremy replied.

"Why?" Sam asked.

Jeremy turned around and stared at him incredulously. After a moment, Sam said, "Oh right. Black kid, nighttime with stolen art work. Got it."

Jeremy shook his head.

"Le Louvre. Let us go to le Louvre," Addie said.

"But it's late," Devon said.

"It is open until nine forty-five on Wednesdays. We still have an hour until closing. Napoleon, can you tell the horse to drop us off near Le Carrousel du Louvre?"

"What's that?" Sam asked.

"That is le Louvre entrance in the underground mall, the one we used the other day. Once we get inside, we can find a place to leave the art."

As they approached the museum, Jeremy could see there were still many people milling about despite the late hour. "Addie, we need to keep away from the lights."

"I will have us land on a back street," Napoleon said. Another whinny, and they descended onto an empty street.

"Tell the horse to wait here for us but to stay out of sight," Jeremy said.

"You expect a horse to stay hidden on the streets of Paris?" Napoleon asked.

"Just tell her. Please."

"Let's go," Devon said.

19. Surprised

The group of four raced down a side street, crossed the square with the large glass pyramid while weaving through a small crowd of people, and ran into Le Carrousel du Louvre. They slowed when they came to an escalator, got on, and descended to the Louvre entrance. Each of them looked around for a spot to put the art, but there wasn't a great option. Small groups of people exited the museum.

"How about over there, behind the seat?" Sam said, pointing.

"Where? On the floor? We can't put the Mona Lisa on the floor," Addie said indignantly.

"Shush, not so loud," Devon said. "How about on that empty bench? I'll put them there, step away, do the magic and we'll leave."

"Okay," Jeremy said. "We'll stand around to block you from view while you take them out."

At the bench, Jeremy, Sam and Addie encircled Devon. Just before he turned to go, Jeremy realized Devon had made a grave error.

"Not the tree!" he whispered loudly. "You can't leave the tree here. Put it back."

"Oh, right," said a flustered Devon. She put the tree back in the backpack and gave it to Addie.

Her face filled with determination, Devon focused on the art. Seconds later the Mona Lisa, the Monet from the Musée D'Orsay, and the Venus de Milo appeared. There was a crash as the bench collapsed under the weight of the statue. Jeremy grimaced as the artworks slid to the floor. He turned and walked away with the others, as cries of surprise erupted behind them.

Once outside, they hurried back to the horse who was busy eating flowers from a flower box. "We need to go to the Eiffel Tower," Jeremy said.

"Do we really need to bother with the tree?" Sam said.

"I have a feeling that yes, we do. And it will only take a few minutes. We're not far away."

They all clambered onto the horse and took off again, ascending only for a moment before descending again.

"There." Jeremy pointed down to the left.

Once they landed, Devon pulled the tree out of the backpack, put it down, closed her eyes, and the tree appeared, its roots firmly set in the ground.

"I thought you'd come back here," said a voice in the shadows.

Jeremy spun around, coming face to face with the man from Portugal. "What do you want?"

"The hat," the man said.

"We want Birdbrain back," Devon said.

"What? This?" He reached into the inside pocket of his jacket and pulled out Birdbrain. "You can have it back when I have that hat."

"And the tower. My city needs the Eiffel Tower back," Addie added.

Without warning, Sam lunged at the man, diving at his legs and tackling him to the ground. After a moment's hesitation, the rest of them joined in. Jeremy wrenched Birdbrain out of his hand, but by this time the man had recovered from his shock of being attacked and was fighting back. In the confusion of arms and legs, the man got to his feet and ran away.

"He's got the hat!" Devon yelled.

"Thing," Jeremy exclaimed, "do your thing!"

"Gladly, but—"

"Please," pleaded Jeremy.

The man suddenly stopped and bounced backwards, having smacked into Thing's invisible wall. He dropped something from his hand but regained his footing and continued on.

Addie ran up to where he had been and picked something up. "It's the tower. He dropped it."

"But he still has the hat," Devon cried, "and he's getting away."

A whinny, followed by a thundering of hooves, startled Jeremy. The carousel horse ran at the man and knocked him off his feet. Sam ran forward and grabbed the hat from the man who appeared dazed and only semiconscious.

Sam ran back to the group. "Come on. Let's do this."

They sprinted to the site of the Eiffel Tower, now dark and deserted. Devon put the miniature tower on the ground, donned the hat, and they all moved a safe distance away. Moments later the Eiffel Tower appeared, the top of its four stories hidden in darkness.

"We better get back to the hotel before our parents send out a search party," Sam said.

"Good idea," Jeremy said.

"Glad this is over," Devon said, taking the hat off. "The sense of power was astonishing, but not in a good way."

Without warning, Devon staggered forward, having been pushed from behind. The man, having regained consciousness and being momentarily forgotten, plowed right into her. He knocked the others aside, snatching the hat from Devon's hand.

"Hey!" Jeremy called out. He started to give chase, but the man had a head start and ran faster, jumping into a taxi. It pulled away from the curb with Jeremy forty feet away. He bent over, trying to catch his breath, and the others came up behind him.

"What now?" Sam said.

They were silent, each of them lost in their own thoughts. Jeremy felt a huge sense of failure, despite all they had done.

"What can we do?" Addie said dispiritedly. "We do not know who he is, he has the hat and ..." Her voice trailed off.

Shouting filled the air. The appearance of the Eiffel Tower, whose lights were beginning to flicker, startled those out for an evening stroll.

"Let's get out of here," Jeremy said. "Quick, while everyone's attention is on the tower. Let's use the horse again."

They jumped on and after walking to a darkened corner, launched into the air one last time. Landing around the corner from their hotel, Jeremy, Devon and Sam called out goodnight to Addie and Napoleon. Birdbrain joined in, but Thing only grumbled incoherently.

"What time is it?" Sam asked.

"Later than you want to know," Devon said.

"What are we going to tell our parents?" Jeremy asked.

"How about that we lost track of time because we were having so much fun, running around with Addie," said Devon. 'We could add something about Paris being so amazing and vibrant and we got sidetracked into a bakery and then—"

"And we also found out about the Sacré-Cœur, how it came back," Sam added.

"We can't tell them what we did," Jeremy said.

"We won't," Sam countered. "We can say we heard people talking, and we went to see it for ourselves. Who can blame us for that? And it would help account for a lot of our time, what with having to wait for the metro. We could say we just missed one train and had to wait what seemed like forever for another one."

"Okay, okay," laughed Jeremy. "I think you guys have it covered."

Their parents weren't as understanding as they'd hoped. At first their parents fussed over them, relieved that they were okay. Once the adults registered that everything was fine and the kids were just late, their concern morphed into anger. But as the kids fumbled out their story, talking over one another, the tension in the room eased, and their parents became more interested in their story of the Sacré-Cœur.

Toward the end of the conversation, Cheryl got up and parted the curtains. "Hey, the Eiffel Tower is back! It's all lit up!"

Jeremy, Devon and Sam all glanced at each other, trying to keep straight faces.

Devon said, "Wow, really? Let's see." And they all strolled to the window.

20. When the Time Comes

The next morning over breakfast in the hotel's restaurant, Devon's dad spoke up. "So what are the plans for today? We've got two days left and our work is done. Any suggestions?"

"Well, our visit to the Louvre was cut short. Would you guys be up to going again?" Cheryl asked, addressing Jeremy, Sam and Devon.

Jeremy shrugged. "Sure. Why not?"

At that moment, Addie approached the table. "Bonjour. Jeremy, Devon, Sam, can I talk to you for a minute?"

As they walked away from the table, Jeremy's mom said, "Those kids are sure having a good time together."

Smiling to himself and seeing a similar grin on Devon's face, Jeremy followed Addie outside where Travis stood waiting for them.

"Addie filled me in on what happened yesterday. It's unfortunate that the man got away with the hat."

"Does anyone know what happened to the other, shorter man?" Devon asked.

"I forgot about him," Jeremy said.

"Tra ... Mr. Davis," Devon started.

"You may call me Travis." He smiled.

"Okay. Um ...Travis. Were there any reports of a statue appearing out of nowhere on a boat?"

"No. But my sources reported this morning that the man stuck under the pillar at the reliquary of Saint Thomas Aquinas has returned."

"You're kidding!" Jeremy exclaimed.

"No, I'm not," Travis replied. "Apparently, the magic that originally put him under the column is binding, and he cannot exist away from the column without the hat."

"Wow," Devon said. "I'm glad I didn't get too attached to that! What if I turned into something—"

"Hey!" Thing interjected. "Watch it!"

"Don't talk to her that way," Birdbrain scolded, flapping her wings at Devon's side.

"Since when do you get to tell me what to do?" Thing pulled on his carabiner trying to get at Birdbrain, but the clip stopped him, and he fell back against Jeremy's leg.

"Since you snapped at—"

A neighing from Napoleon interrupted Birdbrain.

"Guys … enough," Jeremy said.

Sam doubled over with laughter. "Where can I get me one of those?" Sam asked after he caught his breath.

Surprised by the question, Jeremy froze, eying Travis.

The beginnings of a grin disappeared from Travis's face. "Sorry, but I don't have the power to give magic buddies away. Baako does the choosing," Travis replied to the questioning expressions on everyone's faces.

"Who's Baako?" Sam asked.

"Baako is the original magic buddy, and she chooses all who come after her," Travis replied.

"Wait," Thing interjected. "I thought Baako was a he."

"He, she. Does it really matter?" Addie asked.

"Does it really … of course it matters," Thing said.

"Why?" Addie asked.

"Because … it just does."

"Actually, no it doesn't Thing," Jeremy stated, smiling at Addie.

She smiled back before asking, "What kind of name is Baako?"

"West African. It means first born…. So while I cannot give you a magic buddy, Sam, I trust that you will keep what you have witnessed to yourself."

"Of course."

"Good. Okay. Inevitably, the man who got away will use the hat again. We just don't know when or where. When the time comes, we will send you wherever necessary."

"How can you do that? How will you get our parents to agree?" Jeremy's voice trailed off but Devon picked up the thread.

"Oh, I get it. You send our parents where you need us to go, right?"

"Correct."

"Oh, right," Jeremy said. "And sometimes we're actually working on the same case."

"That too," Travis said.

"So, next summer is another adventure," Jeremy said.

"I won't assume it will be next summer. It could be anytime. Those driven by power and greed won't wait for your summer vacation," Travis said.

"Good point," Jeremy said. "Travis, what about that other woman, Heinke, I think her name was? What was that all about? She clearly had bigger plans than taking away the colors of the Golden Gate Bridge."

Travis stood quietly, his eyes on Jeremy. "She did. But unfortunately that is all I am at liberty to say."

"Wait. So you can trust us to run around and solve these mysteries ... no these problems ... but you can't trust us—"

Thing kicked Jeremy in the side. "What? That's a fair question."

"Not that. Your parents are coming."

Everyone turned to watch their parents approach.

"Oh, hi," Travis said. "I ran into your kids, and they were telling me what a great time they've been having. What do you have planned for today?"

"We're going to the Louvre, since it's reopened," Devon's mom said.

"Great," Travis said. "I came to bring you this." He held Jess's backpack out to her. "The police retrieved it after questioning Heinke. I think you'll find that everything is in there, including your passports."

"Oh, that's great. Thank you," Jess said.

"Well, I'm almost late for a meeting," Travis said. "Good-bye and safe travels home."

They all called out their thanks and watched him turn and walk down the street.

"You're going to the Louvre?" Addie said. "What about Disneyland?"

"Wait, what?" Sam said. "There's a Disneyland here?"

"Yes. About an hour away by train."

All of the kids turned and pleaded with their respective parents. Eventually they decided to stick to their plan for the Louvre and go to Disneyland the next day. Addie joined them for both outings.

At one point while they were at Disneyland, Jeremy found himself walking steps behind Devon and Addie, close enough to hear their conversation.

"Are you going to be alright?" Devon said.

"What do you mean?"

"Just that I know it's been hard for you, with your parents."

"Oh, that." They continued along quietly. Jeremy respected how Devon didn't push Addie but let her choose when and how to answer. They turned to watch younger children riding the Dumbo ride. Jeremy stayed off to the side, giving them space.

"I expect we'll work it out," Addie said. "I think Mr. Davis must have told them how I helped find Jeremy and Sam's mom, because they told me they were proud of me the other day. That's something."

Addie turned and smiled at Jeremy. "Do kids give you a hard time because your mom is gay?" she asked.

Jeremy came up next to Addie. "Nah, not really. More so because I'm black and she's white. I've had to learn to ignore people, try and be strong inside ... know who I am and not let anyone take that away from me."

Addie nodded and eyed Jeremy for a moment. She reached out unexpectedly and gave him a hug. After getting over his surprise, he hugged her back.

After the train ride back from Disneyland, Jeremy, Devon and Sam said good-bye to Addie and Napoleon. Birdbrain and Napoleon said a good-bye Jeremy couldn't hear. Thing at least managed to be nice. "Hope you get to fly for real someday," were Thing's parting words.

***

The next day they said good-bye to Paris. Everyone traveled to the airport together. They were all on the same flight to San Francisco where Devon's family would catch a connecting flight to Portland, Oregon. Once at security, the adults were deep in conversation and went ahead, followed by Devon, leaving Jeremy and Sam to go after them. When Jeremy stepped to the front, the security official pulled Jeremy aside for extra screening.

"Hey. Why are you pulling him aside?" Sam said, having gone through security in front of Jeremy. "You know we're both twelve right? Why are you letting me through and not him?"

"It's okay, Sam," Jeremy said, but Sam cut him off.

"No, it's not okay." Sam turned to the security agent who had taken Jeremy. "Hey, that's my bro. You take him, you take me."

Despite his frustration at having yet again been pulled aside, he couldn't help but appreciate Sam's attempts to step up and support him. "Thanks, bro," Jeremy said, giving him a fist bump. "Let's get out of here." They joined their moms who were holding hands, Devon and her parents, and headed off for their flight.

"Pssst."

Jeremy looked down at Thing.

"Where to next?" Thing asked.

Jeremy shrugged, glanced over at Sam and then their moms and with a feeling of acceptance and curiosity, said, "Home."

Epilogue

Knowing he was at school, Thing waddled over to Jeremy's computer and pried it open. He entered Jeremy's password and clicked on the Zoom icon. He started a meeting, sent an invite to Devon, and did jumping jacks while he waited.

Seconds later an image of a stuffed bird, its beak too big for its body and at that moment too close to the screen, popped up.

"Wow, Birdbrain, that's some beak you've got. Don't really need to see it that close up," Thing joked.

"Ha ha. How's this?" she said, moving backward.

"Better."

"Were you doing jumping jacks?" Birdbrain giggled.

"Yeah. Standing around is sooo boring. Anyway, whatcha up to today?"

"Not much. Thought I'd watch some nature documentaries on Devon's computer. And practice moving stuff."

"What do you mean, practice moving stuff?" Thing asked.

"Watch this." Birdbrain stepped back and a book went sliding across the desk in front of her.

"That's awesome. When did you start being able to do that?"

"Just recently. I think it's a new power or something. But I don't quite have the hang of it yet. What about you? Whatcha doing today? Besides finding improved ways of destroying Jeremy's room?"

"How'd you guess?" Thing did a backflip.

"Did he ever get back at you for putting cereal in his bed?"

"Nah. At least not yet. But even if he does, it was so worth it. Nice idea by the way."

"Thanks."

"Why don't you play jokes on Devon?"

"Not my thing," she said with a twinkle in her eye. She paused, waiting for Thing to get the joke.

"Hey, that's not cool!" Thing exclaimed.

Birdbrain chuckled and stood aside as another book went sliding along the table on its own.

ABOUT THE AUTHOR

While she works as a physical therapist, Sussi Voak rises before the sun to follow her writing dreams. This is her second book, and she is currently working on the third in the TDC series. Raised in the Santa Cruz Mountains, Sussi Voak currently lives in Oakland with her son.Visit her author page at www.sussivoak.com, and please consider writing a review on Amazon or Goodreads to help spread the word about this book.

Made in the USA
Las Vegas, NV
29 March 2024